They had called William Drever 'the Copycat Ripper'. He had been convicted of three such crimes and been sentenced accordingly.

So what were the results of this catastrophe for his family? His wife, his children, his parents? This is the world John Wainwright chooses to explore – a world of shame, horror and disbelief: also a world where women are the principal victims and survivors.

Carol Drever, the convicted man's wife, finds herself faced with multiple disasters. She is not made of the metal required to stand these stresses. Other women come to her help. Amid these traumas a very different woman makes an entrance, someone new to the family, unknown – but not, it seems unknown to William Drever.

John Wainwright excels himself in his insight into the life of the family that has suffered a very shocking kind of 'bereavement'. As always the story moves at a great pace – as always there is an ending loaded with surprise. But in this case it is sombre as well.

THE DISTAFF FACTOR

John Wainwright

MACMILLAN LONDON

ISBN 0 333 33601 1

First published 1982 by
MACMILLAN LONDON LIMITED
London and Basingstoke
Associated companies in Auckland Dallas Delhi Dublin
Hong Kong Johannesburg Lagos Manzini Melbourne Nairobi
New York Singapore Tokyo Washington and Zaria

Composition in Plantin by
FILMTYPE SERVICES LIMITED
Scarborough, North Yorkshire

Printed in Great Britain by
THE ANCHOR PRESS LIMITED
Tiptree, Essex

Bound in Great Britain by
WM BRENDON AND SON LIMITED
Tiptree, Essex

Justice treats men as if they were
constantly the same, whether
fasting or well fed, at rest,
euphoric, overworked, or after a
conjugal dispute. Not only is each
one a special case, but each should
be studied at each hour, at each
minute of each day.

When I Was Old
Georges Simenon

She could not forget the eyes. The rest was blurred. Other than the eyes, everything had been out of focus. Vague. Indistinct. Had he been wearing his brown suit? His white shirt and matching brown tie? Had his hair been tidy or had he, as so often in the past, allowed it to flop around without thought of his appearance? She didn't know. She couldn't remember. Perhaps she hadn't even noticed.

As with the scene, so with what had been said. A distant mumble, as if she hadn't been present, but instead had been listening from another room. The jury spokesman; she'd understood his meaning but the actual words had passed her by. The pontification of the judge, the passing of the sentence, the murmur and movement as the court had risen and the three officials had left the high dias; then the pushing and the gentle guiding as the solicitor had escorted her from the court and along the corridors; the press of reporters as they'd left the building, the angry exchange as the solicitor and his clerk had forced a way through to the car.

Nothing. Nothing distinct. Nothing she could *remember*. Nothing she could tell Anne or Robert. Nothing ... and they'd want to know. He was their father, therefore they'd want to know. And she wouldn't be able to tell them, because the only thing she could truly remember was the eyes.

In a gentle voice Rouse said, 'It's all over, Mrs Drever. Relax a little. It's all over.'

'Blue. Real cornflower blue.'

It was her voice which spoke the words. Not deliberately. Not via any conscious effort on her own part. The words were merely the vocal echo of what dominated her mind.

The solicitor frowned and said, 'I beg your pardon?'

'The eyes of a child,' her voice mused. 'Forty-five years old, but the eyes of a child. Children have eyes of that colour. Often. But rarely adults. But *he* has. The eyes of a naughty child, asking for forgiveness.'

'Mrs Drever.' Rouse, the solicitor, cleared his throat. His was a thankless task at moments like this. But he'd chosen Criminal Law as his speciality and this, too, was part of his professional duty. Very tentatively, he stretched out a hand and closed his fingers around the gloved hand of his client's wife. 'Mrs Drever,

7

it has to be faced. He was convicted. Honesty compels me to admit that I wasn't surprised. He'll be an old man when he regains his freedom. He – er – he's always insisted that we accept the verdict. No appeal. It *has* to be faced.'

She bent her head backwards a little and leant the nape of her neck against the cool surface of the car's upholstery. She heard the words. Understood the words. But the eyes continued to dominate her thoughts.

'A rest,' continued Rouse. 'A long rest. Somewhere quiet. Private. Somewhere where you can gradually come to terms with what's happened.'

They'd christened him 'The Copycat Ripper'. When they hadn't known his name; before he'd been identified as William Archibald Drever. The press; the scare-mongers and sensation-seekers; the wicked headline-makers who used their own foul shorthand in order to shock. 'The Black Panther'. 'The York-shire Ripper'. And now 'The Copycat Ripper'.

'Do you have friends somewhere?' asked Rouse. 'Relations, perhaps? Somewhere quiet and out of the way. A month, per-haps. Two months. Until it's been forgotten. Until you can pick up your own life again.'

But he was William. He *wasn't* Peter William Sutcliffe. Noth-ing *like* Peter William Sutcliffe. Not a carbon copy. Not a resur-rection. He was older . . . much older. He hadn't claimed to hear voices. He hadn't made the mistakes Sutcliffe had made; all three had been prostitutes – convicted and rotten with disease. Noth-ing *like* Sutcliffe. Not in looks, not in life-style, not even in the way he'd killed. So why in God's name, 'The Copycat Ripper'?

Rouse's fingers tightened a little and he said, 'I'm trying to help you, Mrs Drever. At this moment you *need* help.'

'How long . . .'

Then the rest of the question stuck in her throat and threatened to choke her. She stared at the roof of the car. The first tears spilled from her eyes and the first hint of trembling quivered through her frame.

'Twenty years, probably less.' Rouse felt the gloved hand gradually clench itself into a fist. 'It's no good ducking the truth, Mrs Drever. Probably less. The chances *are* less. But accept twenty years. Plan accordingly.'

8

'Plan accordingly?'

'You've a life ahead of you. Forty-three? You're a comparatively young woman ... the prime of your life.' He paused, then continued, 'He'd want it. Believe me. I've grown to know him. He'd want you to plan.'

The solicitor's clerk was driving the car. A careful driver. Perhaps too careful. Careful enough to make fellow-drivers impatient. Careful enough to create an accident, without being part of it.

'Did he *say* that?'

'Not in those words. But it's what he'd want.'

The traffic roundabout marked the start of the city's outskirts. The start of the residential district, which would gradually peter out and become open countryside all the way to Beechwood Brook.

The tears flowed more freely now. The dam was cracking and the impossible pressure was being relieved. The shaking, too. As if she was in a fever. But it helped – in some strange, psychological way it helped – and because it helped, because the monumental weight seemed to be slowly easing itself from her shoulders, she felt guilty. Ashamed. She was his wife. They shared things ... *every*thing. The good, the bad ... everything. The good, the bad. Always two halves, always an equal sharing. And now this thing she *couldn't* share. She was letting him down. She should be ...

'A new life.' Rouse was becoming more daring. Choosing his words with less care. 'You're a qualified secretary. Shorthand typist. You'll find work without difficulty. Just – y'know – give it time. Time to heal. Build up a new life. Forget him.'

'Just like that?' she breathed.

'It won't be easy,' admitted Rouse. 'After twenty-three years of marriage. I know it won't be easy.'

Still staring at the roof of the car, still trembling, still allowing the tears freedom to roll down her cheeks, she croaked, 'Go to hell.'

Because doctors equated with sickness, and because she would not admit that her present condition was a form of illness, she had refused to allow a doctor to be called. Rouse had suggested, but hadn't pressed the point; to be told to 'Go to hell' when he'd been doing his best to help and comfort had ruffled his feathers. He *had* done his best in what, from the first, had been a hopeless cause and some degree of credit – some degree of acknowledgement – might have been expected. Instead . . . 'Go to hell'.

So be it.

He'd helped her from the car, bustled her past the handful of rubber-neckers and newspaper people, guided her along the path and into the house. In effect he'd handed her over to her elder sister. Rid himself of a responsibility which, strictly speaking, wasn't his.

'I think you should call a doctor.'

'Yes, I'll do that.'

'I don't *need* a doctor!' And this, despite the continued trembling, the tears still running unheeded down her cheeks; the words almost spat out from behind clenched teeth.

Elizabeth – Elizabeth Stewart, the elder sister – had allowed a sad and tired smile to touch her lips.

Rouse had moved his shoulders, murmured, 'I'll – er – leave her with you. If there's anything you have my office number,' then left.

She'd waited until the door was closed, then said, 'I don't need a doctor, Liz.'

'If you say not.'

'It's shock. That's what it is – most of it – shock.'

'Yes. I suppose so.'

'You've heard the verdict?'

Liz had nodded. As she'd helped her off with her fur coat, she'd added, 'One of the reporters. He came to the door to tell me.'

Still wearing her hat, still wearing her gloves, she'd lowered herself into an armchair. Familar surroundings. The trembling was easing. The tears were slowing. Liz handed her a handkerchief, and she blew her nose loudly and vigorously; as if to reassert the control she claimed over her own emotions. Then she removed her hat, peeled off her gloves and handed them to her elder sister.

'You think not a doctor?' said Liz gently.

'I'm positive not a doctor. A stiff brandy, a couple of aspirins and a hot bath. That's all I need. Then we can talk.'

It was weird. Spooky. It sent spiders crawling up and down Liz Stewart's spine. Carol, she knew, had a will like tempered steel; something to wonder at and at times something almost frightening. But this! The tears were still coming; not as fast, but still trickling down her cheeks. Nor had the trembling quite left her. But no matter. The words were steady. No doctor. Brandy, aspirins and a bath. The normal assertive voice. She, Carol Drever, decided and, having reached a decision, was not open to argument or persuasion ... and nothing was allowed to stand in the way. Not even heartbreak. Where other women – any other woman Liz could think of – would have been grateful for moral support, this younger sister of hers seemed able to stand aside from the mental anguish and order her life coolly and without hesitation.

Liz said, 'I'll run your bath, dear. You'll – er – you might want to telephone Anne and Robert.'

Liz left the room, taking the coat, the hat and the gloves with her.

Carol Drever remained in the chair for a few moments. Fighting herself. Gradually taking control of herself. Then she rose and walked to the drinks cabinet; one step was a little unsteady and she touched the back of the sofa, as if to put confidence into her walk. She unstoppered the brandy decanter, chose a glass and poured herself a drink.

As the neck of the decanter rattled gently against the rim of the glass, she whispered, 'Damn!'

The bath was soothing. If nothing else, she knew her body; knew that a hot soak would ease the tension far sooner and far more completely than any sedative prescribed by some quack. The bath oil scented the water, and the perfumed steam filled the room and condensed on the full-length tinted mirrors.

This bathroom. His birthday present to her on her fortieth birthday. The day so many women fear ... and this despite Miss Tucker's warbled belief.

'More than half-way.'

'What?'

'To the grave. It's all downhill from now on.'

'Rubbish, darling.' That laugh, which was almost a guffaw.

'You're ripe. You'll stay ripe for years.'

'A slightly disgusting way of putting it.'

'The truth. We don't experiment any more. We've learned all the tricks.'

'Why must men always reduce everything to sex?'

'Reduce? Elevate, surely?' Again the near-raucous laugh. 'A birthday present. A ring. A diamond ring. Big enough to be vulgar, right?'

'No.' The slight hesitation, because she didn't want to sound foolish. 'A new bathroom. A very special bathroom.'

And this was it. A *very* special bathroom. The whole works: bath, shower, toilet, bidet and twin wash-basins set into a vanity shelf which ran the full length of one wall. It had cost almost as much as a small house. It hadn't been a matter of extending the existing bathroom; it had needed far more than that. One of the guest bedrooms had been converted. The builders and plumbers had come in from Lessford. The fittings had had to be sent away for . . . from Scotland, somewhere. He'd gone mad. Bevel-edged tinted mirrors from floor to ceiling. Heated rails holding towels big enough to hide under.

And, despite the twin wash-basins, never once had he used this bathroom.

'Yours, darling. All yours and only yours. I'll scrub the muck off in the old place.'

Because he'd known. Cleanliness. Her one weakness which almost amounted to a fetish.

'Dammit, woman, you don't allow yourself time to get even slightly soiled.'

'William, I wish you wouldn't swear.'

'I want a woman. I want you to smell of woman. I've no great yen for a pristine female.'

That was in later years. And yet when they'd married they'd both been virgins. He, awkward and inexperienced; embarrassed and bordering upon the apologetic. So obviously the first time. And she knew damn well *she* was a virgin. That honeymoon! Chaucer could have used it as an addendum to his *Canterbury Tales*. And yet, two decades later . . . this bathroom and "You're ripe. You'll stay ripe for years". The remark of a real man-about-town. Of a mild hellrake. Of William as he'd become, and not

William as he'd once been.

She slid fractionally deeper into the sud-topped water, reached a hand to the centre-placed taps and, as the hot water slowly increased the temperature at her waist, concentrated upon recalling the past, remembering the not-so-distant years and deliberately forgetting the slightly terrifying present.

Liz had percolated freshly ground coffee. It was waiting, along with another stiff brandy, on a low table positioned in front of the glowing bars of the electric fire.

Liz could be relied upon to do those sort of things. Liz, the dependable. Liz, the ex-officio housekeeper who for years had relieved her younger sister of the tedium which normally accompanies the business of being a good wife. A proposed party? A dinner for some influential client and his wife? Tell Liz; she'd arrange for the food, the cooking, the serving and, after it was all over, the clearing away. Liz handled the laundry. Liz carefully checked the bills before handing them over to William for payment. Liz made sure the daily help did her work properly; that the gardener wasn't as shiftless as he'd like to be; that Anne and Robert remembered their parents' birthdays, and sent Thank You notes whenever *they* received presents.

She'd moved in just before Anne was born and had stayed on as permanent baby-sitter. Then Robert had arrived and by that time Liz had become part of the family. She knew them; all four of them. She knew more about them than they knew about themselves; secrets, each would share with her, in the knowledge that the secret would stay untold. She was 'Liz'. Even to the children she was 'Liz'. More than an aunt, more than a sister, more than a sister-in-law. In many ways, she *was* the family; the good cement which held the various pieces together.

As Carol flopped into an armchair, pulled up her feet and tucked the thick bathrobe round her knees, Liz said, 'Feeling better?'

'What would we do without you, Liz?'

'Oh, you'd manage.' Liz handed her sister a tiny cup of black coffee. 'It's sweetened and stirred.' Then, as she took the second cup and settled into the companion armchair, 'What about Anne and Robert?'

'They can stay with their grandmother an extra night.'

'They'll know,' Liz reminded her. She glanced at the expensive carriage clock on the broad, oak mantlepiece. 'The local news. It'll have been on TV. They'll know the verdict by this time.'

'Local?' Carol Drever smiled. A bitter, sardonic curl of the lips. '*National* surely? "The Copycat Ripper". The nation – the world – we're *famous*, Liz. Or should it be infamous?'

'All the more reason for you to ring them. That, at least.'

'Later.' Carol moved a hand and said, 'Get me a cigarette, please.' Liz left her chair, replaced her cup on the table, lifted the cigarette box from the mantlepiece and held it open. She flipped the lighter and held the flame steady. Having replaced the cigarette box, she returned to her chair, and Carol continued, 'What made him do it, Liz? I mean – y'know – *why*?'

'People do things,' murmured Liz. She sipped her coffee. 'Who knows what people think, why they do these silly things?'

'Silly?'

'What would you call it?'

'Evil. What else? Three women. Gutted, like so many rabbits. That's not just *silly*. That's ... foul. And we aren't talking about "people" we're talking about William.'

'We've grown used to it;' observed Liz sadly. 'At first ... remember that first night, when the detective sergeant called and told us they'd arrested him? We stayed up all night. Worrying. Wondering. We were in a terrible state.'

'It was sudden. Unexpected. Carol Drever drew on her cigarette. 'We didn't know why he'd been arrested, and they wouldn't tell us.'

'And when we *did* know. When they *did* tell us. After they'd charged him. It was bad ... but not as bad as that first night.' She sipped coffee before continuing, 'Since then – each time they brought him to the local court for committal – gradually it became part of life. Part of everyday life. And today ...' Again the quick, sad smile. 'Convicted and sentenced, and we sit here drinking coffee. We aren't *really* upset. We've been – I don't know – conditioned. Like somebody suffering a terminal illness. When they die, we're sad but we aren't shocked.'

'I'm shocked,' contradicted Carol Drever. 'Deeply shocked.'

14

'But not distraught.'

'Shocked, though.'

'Ah, but why? Because of what he's done? Because he's been tried and sentenced? Or, perhaps, because they were street women?'

'Everything. It all adds up.'

'And,' insisted Liz, 'when it's all been added up. The sum of it. We can *still* sit here drinking coffee. We can still talk about it without tears.'

'I'd like to know why.' She drained her cup.

'More coffee?'

'No, thanks.' She leaned forward, placed the cup and saucer on the table, and picked up the glass of brandy. She repeated, 'I'd like to know why, if only to be able to understand.'

'Forgive?'

'No . . . not forgive. Never forgive.'

'Because he's a murderer? Because he's a murderer of women? Because he's a murderer of convicted prostitutes?'

'First because he *consorted* with prostitutes. To understand his reason for that might point us in the right direction.'

'Men go with prostitutes,' said Liz simply.

'All men?'

'Some men.' Liz qualified her previous remark.

'All right. Why was he one of them?'

'My dear,' said Liz, gently, 'you're in a position to answer that better than anybody.'

'He needn't,' sighed Carol Drever.

'But he *did*,' insisted Liz.

Their talk was in the past tense. As if he was dead. Long dead and long buried. As if the mourning period was past, and a discussion of the deceased could be indulged in without emotion and without it being ill-mannered.

And in a way this was so. William Archibald Drever had 'died' when the police had explained the reason for his arrest. The three killings had been the stuff of which headlines are made; of a foulness guaranteed to increase circulation.

'God! This bastard's worse than Sutcliffe.'

'I know. I don't want to hear the details. Not over the breakfast table.'

'He's a bloody animal. He's . . .'

'Please, William. Later. When we've eaten.'

And it had been *him* all the time. Him! Going through the motions. Making the outraged remarks expected of him . . . but *him*. In effect, digging his own grave, ready for the moment when he would 'die'. He must have known. He must have known he'd be caught. That having been caught, his wife and family would have to be told. That, at that moment, he would no longer 'belong'. He'd cease to exist. He'd no longer be a husband, or a father, or a son, or a brother, or a brother-in-law . . . or *anything*. As from that moment he'd be 'dead', with no hope whatever of resurrection. He must have known. Whatever else he was – evil, twisted, frustrated, *anything* – he wasn't an idiot, therefore he must have *known*.

'Why?' she breathed. 'In God's name, why?'

Liz didn't answer. Instead, she rose from her chair, having placed her cup and saucer on the table, and walked to the high window. The October dusk was thickening into darkness. The start of a night mist was being caught and held by the lower branches of the trees.

She said, 'Some of them are still there.'

'Who?'

'The newspaper people.'

'Vultures.' Sneering contempt gave the word added meaning.

'Their job,' sighed Liz. 'Before we knew it was William, we were eager to read the latest details.'

'What more do they want? They know it all now. What else can they ask?'

'I think they call it "the human angle".'

She closed the heavy velvet curtains and for a moment – until she switched on the lights – the illumination from the electric fire made the room a place of scarlets and blacks. On her way back to the armchair the telephone rang. She swerved course to answer it.

'Yes . . . Who's speaking? . . . I'm sorry that's not possible . . . She's in no condition to answer the telephone . . . No, most certainly not . . . I'm her sister, if it's any business of yours . . . No, nothing . . . Look, will you please leave us alone!'

She slammed the receiver back onto its rest, and said, 'Another newspaper-man.'

Carol Drever said, 'Leave it off the hook.'

Liz hesitated a moment, then lifted the receiver from its prongs and rested it on the surface of the telephone table. Before she resumed her seat she, too, took a cigarette from the box and lighted it.

There seemed nothing to say. Nothing worth saying. Everything had *been* said; said a dozen times over and in varying sorts of ways.

In God's name, why William? A very ordinary, run-of-the-mill man. Ambitious, perhaps. Hard working. Different from the young man she'd first met and fallen in love with, but, God, that was almost thirty years ago, and, in some ways, he *had* to be different. Shy, unsure of himself then; a newly certified accountant gazing, owl-eyed around him looking for some promising opening, something with 'prospects'. Today a director of an up-and-coming firm; a member of the town's professional clique; the head of a two-car, two-house family. As different as *that*. But, basically, the same man.

And yet ... a monster!

That a man could *be* a monster and look so ordinary – so everyday, so pleasant, so clean-looking and (yes) so *good*-looking – it was all wrong. Oscar Wilde had got it all wrong. *The Picture of Dorian Gray*. Evil *doesn't* have an outward appearance. It *doesn't* show itself. No boils, no superating sores, no red-rimmed and staring eyes. Nothing. Not Dorian Gray, but Willam Archibald Drever, provincial man-about-town and looking the part, but also the personification of evil. A sadist. A lecher. A butcher. Not merely a killer, a mutilator, but a very pleasant companion. A nice chap with whom to share a round of golf. A friendly fellow and just the sort to ask to dinner and an evening's conviviality. Popular, and rightly so. A great guy ... who screwed whores in secret and, having screwed them, slit them open from crotch to sternum.

'The blood,' she murmured. 'I still can't understand about the blood.'

'What?' Liz jerked herself from her own thoughts.

Carol Drever uncurled herself, stood up and took another cigarette from the box on the mantlepiece.

As she lighted it she said in a steady voice, 'He must have been literally bathed in blood. Why didn't we ever *notice* anything?'

'My dear, I don't think we should dwell . . .'

'I *want* to "dwell".' The interruption might have been touched with hysteria. 'What else should we think about? What else *can* we think about? What he did to those women. There must have been blood everywhere.'

'He . . .' Liz moistened her lips. 'The police explained. He included it in his statement, so they said.'

'That he bathed?' She resumed her curled up position in the armchair.

'So it would seem.'

'That he was naked when he used his knife on them?'

'Y-yes. So – so it would seem.'

'You realise exactly what that means?'

'For God's sake Carol!'

'What everybody who's read that tit-bit of information will have asked themselves?'

'No more, *please*.'

'Where in hell's name did he hide the knife?'

Liz dropped her head, raised her hands and covered her face with her hands.

'*I* know. *You* know. I was in court when the whole sordid story was made public. That he undressed in another room. That having used the woman, he excused himself. The toilet. To relieve his bladder. That he returned with the knife. *But that's never been included in a newspaper report.* I've never seen it. Have you?'

Without moving her hands Liz shook her head.

'A dirty joke, see?' The hysteria was gradually mounting. 'He's been turned into a dirty joke. Where he hid the knife. Some blue comedian will have already worked out a punch line. Some filthy-minded audience will have already . . .'

'Carol! If you don't shut up, instantly, I'll leave this room.'

'He's *not* a dirty joke.' With the speed of a flipped coin the hysteria turned into tight-jawed rage. 'To me, to us . . . my God, to *us* he's not funny. Not funny. Foul. Disgusting. But he's out of it. He's locked away behind high walls. It won't affect *him*. You think that's fair? You think that's . . .'

'Shut up!' Liz lowered her hands. The tears stained her cheeks and her eyes were angry, but the anger was a different anger to that of her sister's. 'What he did . . . it's unforgiveable. All right. It's unforgiveable. But to us he was a good man. A good husband. A good father. A good man. There was something we couldn't understand. That's all. A secret he couldn't share. Blame him by all means. Blame him for what he did. But don't blame him for how the newspapers reported it. Don't blame him for *everything*. Don't understand. Don't even try to understand. But don't condemn him for things he can't control.'

'Don't understand? Don't *understand*? Who the hell can understand a monster?'

Liz's lips trembled slightly as she said, 'Who knows? The person who created it perhaps?'

Elizabeth and Carol Stewart. They were typical, in that they represented the majority of sisters; their personal relationship was that strange love-hate mixture shared by the vast majority of their kind.

As children their chosen playmates had been made up of different groups. As teenagers they had each had their own 'best-friend'; to an extent they had each gone their own way, lived their own lives and, had they not been sisters, the chances are they would not even have been friends. But they were sisters and, with growing maturity, the friendship had developed into something far more than a family necessity. But a friendship peculiar to sisters. A friendship which pulled no punches; which at times could spawn a deliberate hurt or a deliberate insult. And yet, however deep the hurt, however wounding the insult, the friendship was strong enough to carry it and survive.

Carol's marriage had strengthened the friendship; the fact that they no longer lived under the same roof, and saw each other less, tempered an already steel-strong bond. And Liz had moved in, then Anne had been born, then Robert, and when, five and seven years later, their father then their mother had died there had been an unspoken but understood offer and acceptance. The Drever's home was Liz's home.

Even the armchair she was sitting in. It wasn't 'her' chair – nothing as hidebound as that – but it was the chair she favoured and as a result it was often left unoccupied, even when she wasn't present and wasn't expected for some time.

Carol sniffed back the tears.

Liz fished a tiny handkerchief from her sleeve, blew her nose, then muttered, 'That was a wicked thing to say. I'm sorry.'

'We're on edge.' Carol was even prepared to make excuses for her elder sister. 'Both of us. We have to be careful. We've only each other now.'

She meant the words. She meant them as she spoke them but, although she didn't realise it, they were born of mutual self-pity. The mix of emotions precluded any hope of logical thought. Had she been asked, she would not have hesitated. She hated her husband. She loathed him, detested him and would, for the rest of her days, feel unclean because she had allowed him to enter her body. She would have claimed that, she would have believed it, but she would have been wrong. Love cannot be turned off like a tap; it can be denied and with time it can die . . . but not suddenly. Not instantaneously. Too much of her life had been his life, too much of his life had been hers. The hatred would come. Given time, and if she worked at it hard enough, the hatred she claimed would be hers. But not easily and not overnight. Not even in weeks or months. It would take years.

That was part of her suffering. She yearned for something still well beyond her reach. She claimed what she did not yet have.

The front doorbell rang.

Liz rose from her chair and said, 'I'll go.'

'If it's a reporter, warn him I'll have the police round.'

'I'll handle it.'

But it wasn't a reporter. It was William's colleague, Samuel Jones.

Some men have what is colloquially known as 'a presence'. What Hollywood, in its dream factory days, called 'star quality'. They enter a room, and there is an immediate optical illusion; the dimensions of the room seem to lessen. They seem to take up more than their fair share of space.

Nor does the physical size of the man matter. Jones was not a big man – in stocking feet he barely topped the five-nine mark – and yet because he had 'presence' the impression was that he was a friendly, sombre-faced giant. He wore a dark overcoat against the evening chill. He carried a trilby and gloves in one hand. His hair was silver-white and immaculately groomed. He was the power-house behind the firm of which William had been a director and, little more than a year back he'd been awarded an MBE for services to small industries.

Liz waved him towards an empty chair.

Jones said, 'No, thank you. I'll stand.'

'A drink? Coffee, perhaps? I was thinking of making some fresh. Or something stronger?'

'Nothing, thank you.'

Orchestrally speaking, his voice was double-bass played by a virtuoso; it had depth, strength, resonance, but at the same time it could be gentle. It was gentle now as he spoke directly to Carol Drever.

'I heard the news. The verdict.'

She nodded.

'I'm sorry. It's beyond my comprehension – well beyond my comprehension – but it seemed right and proper to await the outcome of the trial.'

He paused, then continued, 'I'm here to add to your sorrow, Mrs Drever. I'm sorry about that, too.'

She frowned non-understanding and said, 'Please ... sit down.'

For a moment he seemed undecided, then he said, 'Thank you,' and lowered himself into Liz's chair. He placed his hat and gloves carefully on the carpet before crossing his legs, linking his fingers and continuing.

'William – I don't have to tell you – was on the board of directors. Financial Director. That was his official nomenclature. I nominated him. It seemed a good idea at the time. It was the biggest mistake I ever made.'

'He was a good accountant.' This she didn't know, accountancy was a closed book to her, but she found herself defending a husband who a few moments before she'd been mentally cursing.

'Too good an accountant.' Jones smiled a tight, hard smile. 'He had a way with figures. He could make a balance sheet say whatever he wanted it to say.'

'I'm sorry, I don't . . .'

'He was a scoundrel, Mrs Drever. Over the years – over the last ten years – he's systematically filched money from the firm. A lot of money.'

'Oh, my God!'

Liz closed her eyes for a moment, then stretched out a hand to touch the mantlepiece, as if to steady herself.

Jones continued, 'We had our suspicions. There was an independent audit. We discovered what he'd been doing just before . . .' Jones cleared his throat. 'Just before this other thing came to light. The sum was too large. The firm couldn't carry it. We had a choice. To prosecute or to come to some arrangement.'

'What sort of arrangement?' whispered Carol Drever.

'If we'd prosecuted he'd have gone to prison. We had proof, you see. He'd have gone to prison. But that wouldn't have got our money back. So we came to an arrangement.'

Carol Drever repeated, 'What sort of arrangement?'

'The sum wasn't small.' Jones seemed to be apologising for what he was about to say. 'I don't want to add to your present worries, Mrs Drever. But you must have realised something. This house. The cottage on the Cornish coast. Your general life style. All on the salary William was being paid. A little thought, that's all. It can't be done.'

Very softly, Liz said, 'How much?'

'Seventy thousand – near enough – a round figure.'

For a third time, Carol Drever said, 'What sort of arrangement?'

'This house and its contents. In effect, he transferred it to the firm.

'That's – that's *ridiculous*!'

'No, Mrs Drever. I'm afraid it's legal. It doesn't belong to William any more. Nothing. He was merely allowed the use of it pending him finding employment elsewhere. We – er – we didn't want to be too harsh . . . despite what he'd done.'

'I don't believe you. He'd have told me. He'd have . . .'

'Mrs Drever.' The interruption was gentle, but firm. 'I wish I hadn't had to come on this errand. He didn't *want* you to know. That was an assurance he asked us to give . . . not to tell you. As far as we were concerned it meant nothing either way. He could tell you his own version. That's why we've waited until his conviction for the other thing. An acquittal . . .' Jones moved his hands, expressively. 'He could have continued looking for somewhere else.'

Jones waited for a reaction. It was slow in coming, and when it came it had a flat, somnambulistic quality.

'This house doesn't belong to me?'

'I'm afraid not.'

'The furniture? The cars?'

'I'm sorry.'

'The Cornish cottage?'

'That's still yours, Mrs Drever. You've still somewhere to live.'

'Money? The bank account?'

'He's on overdraft,' sighed Jones.

Liz seemed to have pulled herself together. She looked worried, but not dazed.

'How long?' she asked softly.

'I beg your pardon?'

'Before you want us out?'

Jones looked uncomfortable, then said, 'The original period – the period we gave William – was a year. I see no reason to alter that time span.'

So that was it. Murderer *and* thief. Lecher *and* cooker of books.

Carol Drever felt distinctly punch drunk. Jones had left, Liz had returned to the chair, they'd both tippled one more glass of brandy and were sitting in silent company with their thoughts.

Jones's visit had explained at least two things. Unimportant things, but things she hadn't understood. Rouse's remark about her being a qualified shorthand typist; that she'd find work without too much difficulty. At the time it had seemed an empty, slightly silly piece of meaningless comfort. But he'd known about this other thing. He'd known and, in his own clumsy way, he'd tried to prepare her. But it wouldn't be that easy. Rouse was out of touch with reality. God knew how long it was since she'd sat at a typewriter; since she'd taken pad and pencil to record in shorthand. The unhappy truth? That any teenager, straight from a tin-pot secretarial college was a better shorthand/typist than she was these days. The knack goes. The skill leaves you. Like a musician; stay away from the instrument long enough, and although you still know the 'how', the practical application is no longer there.

And the eyes. The pleading for forgiveness. William knew. Too damn right he knew! The other thing – the prostitute thing – that was only part of it. It was *this* he was ashamed of. Leaving his wife and children destitute. Not even 'clean' thieving; not stealing, banking the proceeds and, at least, leaving his family with enough cash to live on; fiddling the books, over-spending, living the high life ... then leaving his responsibilities outside while he lived in spartan comfort in some prison.

Sure, he could afford outrageously extravagant bathrooms. Sure, he could take them on expensive, luxury holidays twice, sometimes three times, a year. Sure, he could run two houses, two cars, have a wardrobe of fine clothes, drink only the best booze. Sure, he could live high, wide and handsome. When the final account was presented he wasn't going to be around to pay.

She muttered, 'Jesus, he was a real bastard.'

'We have to eat.' Liz allowed her natural practicality to come to the fore. 'We can't weep on empty stomachs.'

'I'm not hungry.'

'Nor I. But when was your last meal?'

'I had breakfast.'

'That's what I mean. We have to eat.'

'Liz.' Carol Drever eyed her elder sister with suspicious hostility. 'So far you haven't criticised him. Not once.'

'Why should I?'

'For God's sake! He's the louse to end all lice. He's ...'

'He's given me a home. A *good* home.'

'It wasn't his to give.'

'All right, but I've taken it and enjoyed it. I'm grateful.

'He's a – he's a ...'

'I know exactly what he is. What the world will call him. To me he's been a damn good meal ticket.'

'We've nowhere. We've nothing.' The eyes blazed. The words were almost shouted. 'Hasn't that sunk in? He's left us holding the messiest baby in creation ... and he doesn't give a damn.'

'I'm going to raid the fridge. I'll be back.' The tone was low but harsh, controlled and forced from behind clenched teeth and stiff lips.

'I don't want anything. I couldn't . . .'

'You'll eat.'

'The hell I'll eat. It would choke me.'

'You'll eat,' snapped Liz. 'You'll eat and be glad you *can* eat. Three women can't . . . or have you forgotten them? I don't care a button about what he's pinched from the firm. When I've heard his side I'll make judgement. Maybe they asked for it. Maybe he's not the only one . . . the whipping-boy for others. I'll make up my mind when he's explained things. Meanwhile, we've a year. We might not *live* a year . . . that would be a very neat solution to everything. But while we live I owe him something. To look after you. To look after Anne and Robert. That's a debt I intend to pay.'

She turned and marched stiff-backed from the room.

The jury, having reached a verdict, had returned to their homes and taken up their respective lives at the point at which the tiny interruption had occurred. The judge, having pronounced sentence, had taxied back to his hotel, bathed, changed and was enjoying a pre-dinner cigar. The various court officials – the clerks, the barristers, the solicitors – had doffed their wigs, removed their gowns, closed their brief-cases and were enjoying each his, or her, form of off-duty relaxation. Even William Archibald Drever. Prior to the conviction and sentence, the holding prison had treated him more as a guest than an inmate, but now the rigmarole of being transformed from free citizen to convicted murderer robbed him of time to think or feel sorry for himself.

In short, those within the machine were not going slowly mad.

They were fortunate. Temporarily even William Archibald Drever was fortunate. But Carol Drever and Elizabeth Stewart were not so fortunate. They sat before the electric fire, nibbled at cold chicken, potato salad, and buttered wholemeal bread, drank hot, sweet tea from hand-made beakers . . . and tasted nothing. The room was warm. Outside the early night was baring the first fangs of winter's frost, but the central heating, backed by the glowing bars of the fire, kept the temperature of the room cosy and comfortable.

And yet they were cold. It was a coldness born of a numbness. Carol Drever had experienced it on the drive back to Beechwood Brook; she'd been in court, she'd witnessed at first hand the high point of a murder trial, with her husband in the dock and sentenced. Back at home, anger and outrage had taken over for a while and warmed her. The visit of Jones, and what he'd said, had countered the shock. To understand was to think; to be furious required some degree of emotion. But now numbness had taken over. What the medics might have called 'secondary shock' ... and her blood seemed to be cooling in her veins. The trembling threatened to start up again, and her face was the colour of old parchment, kept hidden in some dark cupboard for centuries.

Nor was Liz much better. With her it was the growing realisation. Her normal, down-to-earth temperament had been battered into submission. She'd tried ... God, how she'd tried! Somebody had to remain level-headed; scores of times, she'd clenched her teeth and silently told herself that that was *her* job. Somebody *hadn't* to panic. Somebody had to remain in control of the situation and, in so doing, rescue whatever was possible from the wreck of lives of people less able to cope than herself.

But the numbness was creeping over her, too. What on earth *could* be rescued? William really *was* a monster. On the face of it he'd done far more than butcher a trio of whores. As an addendum he'd deliberately ruined all chances of his own family ever starting a new life. He'd *really* scuttled the ship. His wife – his children – he'd ripped all hope from their grasp. They were just about penniless – no home, no job, no anything – and for starters the legal fees would be coming in very soon. In God's name why, William? In God's name why? You were selfish. We knew that. Carol and I both knew you were selfish. Not at first, perhaps. Not when we first knew you. Then you were unsure. You didn't know what lay ahead. You couldn't afford to be selfish. You were too frightened to be selfish. But later ... Success changed you. Oh, how it changed you! Like so many people, you mistook greed for ambition.

'Liz, I'm going to get to the top. The very top.'

'I hope so.'

'Not hope. Determination. Hoping's no good. You have to act.'

'As long as the price isn't too high.'

'No price is too high, Liz. Not for what I'm after. Up there at the top of the tree. Plums, Liz. Fat, juicy plums. Mine for the picking. Mine for the eating. And I'm *going* to eat them ... every last one of them. Not to be shared. With *anybody*.'

Remember that conversation, William? Remember that statement of belief? It frightened me. It frightened me then, it frightens me still. It stank of megalomania. I was frightened for Carol. I was frightened for Anne and Robert. I was frightened for *you*. Megalomania and self-destruction were in those words. I knew it even then. All you've done is prove me right.

Well, how do the plums taste, now you're in a cell? How did they taste while you were rutting women of the street? When you ripped them open and spilled their guts? Was *that* necessary before you could sink your teeth into your plums? Was *that* part of the price you were prepared to pay?

One part of her mind registered the sound of a car approaching then stopping. The sound of car doors being opened and closed. The soft babble of voices.

The doorbell rang.

Carol said, 'If that's another damn reporter ...'

'I'll go.'

It wasn't a reporter. It was William's parents with Anne and Robert.

They were very much alike; chunky, elderly, soberly dressed, iron grey hair trimmed in a no-nonsense style. They could have been brother and sister. Twins even. They were typical Yorkshire. 'Country' Yorkshire. Florid of face and blunt to a point bordering upon rudeness.

Bill and Mary Drever. The parents of a monster, but ready to go to their grave denying that he *was* a monster. They ushered Anne and Robert Drever ahead of them and they in turn were followed into the room by Liz. Liz closed the door and followed them slowly towards the hearth.

Twenty-year-old Anne seemed to hesitate for a moment, then she rushed towards her mother, dropped to her knees alongside the armchair, flung her arms around Carol Drever's neck and throbbed as the sobs shook her whole body. Carol stroked her daughter's hair and crooned comforting noises. The son, Robert, looked embarrassed at his sister's outpouring of emotion; eighteen years old, he had his father's one-time awkwardness. He stepped aside to allow his grandparents to pass.

Mary Drever said, 'We've been trying to get in touch.'

'The phone's off the hook.' Carol looked up, long enough to offer an explanation, then resumed the comforting of her daughter.

Bill Drever growled, 'You should have got in touch. Dammit, we've been out of our minds.'

'The children,' added his wife. 'They haven't known what to think.'

Liz moved farther into the room, and said, 'Sit down, Mrs Drever. Mr Drever.' She forced a sad smile. 'The reporters. They've been a nuisance. That's why we removed the receiver.'

Get 'em shifted,' said Drever. 'Phone the police. Get 'em shifted.'

'For the moment,' said Liz gently, 'the police aren't exactly on our side.'

Drever sniffed and lowered himself onto the sofa. His wife (it seemed quite deliberately) claimed the chair Liz usually used. Robert shoved his hands into his trouser pockets, muttered, 'It's all right. I'm all right,' and remained standing.

Liz said, 'I'll – er – I'll brew some more tea. Make some sandwiches,' and left the room.

For a few moments, Carol Drever consoled her daughter, then said, 'That's it, pet. We – y'know – we have to talk. I know how you feel. How we all feel. Dry your eyes, darling.'

Anne nodded into her mother's shoulder, then took the proffered handkerchief, dabbed her face and curled up on the carpet alongside her mother's chair.

'Well?'

Mary Drever spoke the word. It hit the short silence, like a starter's pistol; the signal to begin ... whatever was about to begin.

'Did you go?' asked Bill Drever gruffly.

'Of course.'

Mary Drever said, 'It wouldn't help. You being there. He'd be upset.'

'Yes.' Carol Drever tried to keep the sarcasm from her tone. 'He was upset.'

'You being there wouldn't help.'

'My being there – my *not* being there – it didn't make a scrap of difference.'

'He was *my* son. I gave him life . . .'

'Oh, my God!'

'. . . I know him better than anybody on earth. I brought him up, from when he was a bairn. Whenever he was poorly – and he was a poorly child – it was *me* . . .'

'Mother-in-law.' All the years of suppressed antagonism went into the harsh interruption. It bordered on a soft scream of pent-up hatred. Then the tone almost quivered with rage and she went on, 'While you were "bringing him up" why didn't you teach him common decency? Why didn't you point out that cross-screwing doesn't make for a happy marriage? That killing whores isn't on a par with Ludo? That shoving your hand in the nearest till isn't the done thing?'

'What the hell's that supposed to mean?' snarled Bill Drever.

She told them. Oh, how she told them and enjoyed telling them. How she flavoured each word and delighted in the taste of each phrase. 'Nothing small, you understand. Nothing fiddling and unimportant for dear William. Seventy thousand. More than he had or ever would have. More than he could ever repay.' She ignored the presence of Anne and Robert; that she was deliberately emphasising the foulness of their father was for the moment of no importance. The parents of the man who had shamed her – the people responsible for him being born – the in-laws who had over the years, by implication and innuendo, left no doubt that they held the belief that their precious son could so easily have chosen a better wife. 'Not a penny. Not a brass farthing. Something else you "brought him up" to believe in, no doubt.'

For more than five minutes she tore into them. Riding them, trampling them, hurting them. The elderly couple who could have taken over as second-best-parents when her own parents had died, but who hadn't even tried. The nearest thing she could get to William himself. The closest she could come to spitting venom at the man *really* responsible.

It was ugly. It was cheapening. But it was also inevitable. The hurt was too deep for it to be otherwise. Her own personality insisted that she force them to share the heartbreak.

The sheer passion of her outburst left her panting. Her face had the sheen of perspiration and a hint of spittle ran from one corner of her mouth.

'And that's it,' she ended. 'That's the precious son you "brought up" so well. I hope you're proud of him.'

Bill Drever forced himself to croak, 'We'd best go. We're not needed here, mother.'

His wife was shaking and unable to speak.

'Come on, Mother. We've our own home to go to.'

He pushed himself to his feet, helped his wife to stand then, still holding her elbow to steady her, led her from the room. They walked as if they'd both had a little too much to drink.

Carol Drever sucked in deep breaths. She wiped her lips with the back of one hand. Then in a steadier, calmer voice, she said, 'Robert. Reach me a cigarette, please.'

'No.'

He was eighteen and eighteen is a terrible age. A betwixt-and-between age. Not young, but not yet old enough. A black-and-white age; an age lacking in experience and over-filled with beliefs. By any yardstick, one hell of an age at which to meet this brand of domestic upheaval.

He swallowed, then almost groaned, 'I'm ashamed of you, Mother. You shouldn't have said those things to Grandma and Gramp. She's been crying almost all day. *He's* cried. It was awful to watch them. And then you . . .' He closed his mouth, blinked, then ended, 'I'm going to bed.'

Still with his hands in his pockets, he turned and walked from the room, heeling the partly-open door wide and not pausing to close it.

'Anne, darling?'

There was soft desperation in the words. She could have moved from the armchair and reached for the cigarette herself, but the cigarette was unimportant. The cigarette was merely the excuse for the plea. The entreaty.

Stone-faced and stiff-limbed, the daughter pushed herself from the carpet, took the single step necessary to bring her close enough to the mantlepiece, then reached cigarette box and lighter and placed them carefully on her mother's lap.

Carol Drever nodded her thanks. For the moment, she couldn't trust herself to speak.

Anne bent and touched her mother's cheeks with her lips. Cold lips, and a mere touching; an acknowledgement rather than a kiss.

'Me too, mother.'

'What?'

'Bed. Goodnight.'

With Anne it was as if she was walking a narrow plank; her eyes gazed at the carpet less than a hand's-span in front of her shoes. She looked up only when she reached the door. Liz stood aside to let her pass.

'Goodnight, Liz.'

'Goodnight Anne, my pet.'

Liz closed the door with her bottom and carried the tray to the table. A small plate of sandwiches, a tea-pot, milk, sugar, four cups and four saucers filled the tray.

As she poured Liz murmured, 'Too many, even now.'

'What?'

'Anne and Robert.' She handed milked and sweetened tea to Carol Drever. 'I'll see if they want hot chocolate later.'

Liz lighted a cigarette before she settled in her own chair. For a few moments they chewed sandwiches, sipped tea and smoked in silence.

Then, almost off-handedly, Liz remarked, 'Quite a performance.'

'You heard?'

'Oh, yes. I didn't even have to listen. At a guess half Beechwood Brook heard.'

'It needed saying.'

'No, my pet. You needed to say it . . . not quite the same thing.'

'Don't psychoanalyse me,' muttered Carol.

'I don't have to.' Liz's smile was sad. 'You're a bitch, darling. A spoiled and selfish bitch. It's your nature. You can't help yourself.'

It was past midnight – well past midnight – and the October rain soaked the world in a silent, steady drizzle. As if the heavens themselves were weeping at the present wretchedness. Liz lay on her side and, in the wash of nearby street-lighting, watched the moisture slide down the panes of the window. Behind her she could feel the tiny movement as Anne pretended to be asleep; the rise and fall of her breathing; the occasional twitch of a limb seeking to stave off cramp. The younger woman had been there when she'd arrived from downstairs. 'Can I sleep with you tonight Liz, please?' 'Of course, my pet. I need somebody, too.' But sleep hadn't come, and each remained as motionless as possible in order not to disturb the other. A mutual charade of rest, when rest was impossible with the thoughts and emotions racing through their brains.

God, what a mess! What an unholy mess! Robert, only a few yards away, in the darkness of his own room, nursing his own mix of dark thoughts and personal shame. Alone because he was a 'man'. Unable to share, but not yet old enough to carry such a burden. Because he was the son, slightly favoured by his parents and the apple of his grandmother's eye. He needed comforting, but the rules of the game prohibited the giving of comfort. Unable to enjoy the luxury of tears, because 'men' (other than 'old men' like his grandfather) were forbidden such weaknesses. Liz knew Robert; knew his standards and knew his youthful principles. Unattainable standards and impossible principles. But that was a truth he had yet to learn, and was in the process of learning. Poor Robert. Of them all, nobody was suffering more than he was.

And Anne. There, alongside her, pretending to be asleep. In textbook jargon, long past puberty but in fact still a child. Still with the innocence of childhood. 'Liz, when I grow up, I want to be like you. Show me, please.' And that remark made less than two years ago. 'Anne, my pet, you'll grow up like yourself. We all do. We're all unique.' 'Yes, but like you more than like *any-body*.' 'Your mother, pet.' Loyalty had demanded the gentle rebuke. 'Be like her. You'll be a nice person.' But it had been her aunt she'd wanted to sleep with. Not her mother. Unable to face the darkness alone. Unable to handle things without the support of her beloved Liz.

My God, William, you've a lot to answer for, and not all of it in a court of law. Most of it *not* in a court of law. Tomorrow's breakfast headlines. Today has only been a taste. The *hors d'œuvre*. The full meal has yet to come. We haven't yet *seen* the banquet. I wonder if you thought of that, when you ...

'Listen!' Anne sat up in bed as her exclamation cut into Liz's thoughts.

'The cistern. The hot water cistern.'

Liz strained her ears, then said, 'It's only somebody ...'

'It's not Robert. I'd have heard him. There's a squeaking board in the passage.'

'All right,' soothed Liz. 'It's your mother. Perhaps she ...'

'She always uses her own bathroom. *Always*. And it's not that cistern.'

Something of the younger woman's urgency reached Liz. She swung out of bed, switched on the light and threw a dressing-gown over her shoulders. She led the way from the bedroom, along the passage and, without pausing to knock opened the door of the master bedroom. The light from the en suite bathroom on the left – the original en suite bathroom, which William had always used – spilled into the bedroom, and the nightgowned figure was there, leaning over the washbasin, slashing away with a safety-razor blade at her left wrist. Steam from the hot tap billowed upwards and, already, scarlet splashed on the porcelain and dripped onto the white carpet.

'Nine-nine-nine,' snapped Liz.

'Oh, my God! She's ...'

'Don't argue, child. Get an ambulance. Then tell Robert.'

Anne turned and ran back along the passage. Liz almost ran into the bathroom, grasped the shoulder of her younger sister and swung her round from the washbasin. The face was contorted and ugly with heartbreak and self-pity and, even as she turned, she made another slash at her wrist. The fury of the open-handed slap across the face sent Carol sprawling and, as she fell, the blade flew from her fingers.

Liz gasped, 'You – you bloody *cow*!' grabbed a towel and for a moment fought her sister then, as all opposition disappeared, bound the towel with tight savagery around the opened wrist.

33

Enemies are, to me, as important as friends in my life, and when they die I mourn their passing.

Making Of A Muckraker
Jessica Mitford

'She'll live.' The medic's name was Bryant; late-forties, angular, going both bald and grey. He was of the old school – typical family G.P. whose turn it was to be on call for emergencies at Beechwood Brook Cottage Hospital – and, although the latest electronic medical gadgetry would have left him baffled, the impression was that when it came to life-and-death surgery, performed with a bread-knife on the nearest kitchen table, he was the lad to have around. He clicked his tongue and said, 'Silly lass. All she's done is make more worry for herself.'

'You know the history?' said Liz gently.

'Sister told me.' He eyed the woman with the wild hair and the dressing-gown over her nightdress. 'You're the mother-substitute, I take it?'

'I came in with her.'

'And her son and daughter?'

'They came in the car. I sent them home when we knew things were going to be all right.'

'Things will be all right.' He glanced at the sleeping figure in the side-ward bed. His glance touched the bandaged arm, with the drip-tube running to the plastic bag. 'If ever you have the same idea, don't try *that* way. It never works. It takes too long ... somebody always arrives in time.'

'Is she ...' Liz fished around for the right expression. 'Under sedation?'

'Up to the eyeballs in dope,' he assured her. 'She'll sleep solid till this evening. Wake up, have a snack, then go to sleep again.'

'She's taken a beating.'

'I can imagine. Why wasn't her doctor called before?'

'She wouldn't hear of it.'

'I can imagine that, too.' He reached out a hand and grasped Liz firmly by the elbow. 'And now, *you* go back to bed.'

'I'd rather ...'

'Doctor's orders, lassie.'

'You're not my doctor,' she protested weakly. She looked down at the sleeping figure of Carol Drever; at the sweat-damped hair and the bloodless lips and the dark-socketed eyes. 'She needs somebody to be here when she comes round.'

'Somebody *will* be here.' He smiled, and the smile seemed to give youth to his middle-aged face. 'We run a very efficient

37

hospital here. Not quite Guy's, but we know how to feed 'em and comfort 'em.'

She allowed herself to be guided from the side-ward. Along the corridors and out into the tiny parking lot. 'I'll run you back. It's not too far out of my way.' Nor did she raise objection when he helped her into the front passenger seat of the Peugeot. She was too tired to raise objections. Too emotionally drained. One person could carry the worries of the world for only so long . . . after that, the hell with everything.

It was a short ride and a silent one. He drove carefully. He even steered to avoid potholes and badly patched surface repairs; he was aware of her bone-weariness, and for the moment she was his patient and the ride was part of the treatment. He braked gently at the gate, climbed from the car and held the door open for her.

'Bed,' he reminded her.

She nodded.

'See her this afternoon,' he suggested. 'Later this afternoon. About four o'clock. She'll still be dopey but compos mentis.'

Again she nodded, and he watched her as she dragged her way towards the door.

Anne met her at the door. Anne had bathed and dressed and, for the moment, roles were changed. The twenty-year-old nodded thanks to the watching Bryant, then closed the door and guided Liz up the stairs and into the bedroom.

Robert Drever had an ambition; it filled his whole waking life, and took much of the pocket money his father (and now his mother) allowed him. Where other eighteen-year-olds pulled the birds, or fantasised about ton-up M.V.-Agustas, or yelled themselves hoarse in encouragement of eleven shirted heroes on a football pitch, Robert Drever dreamed of being an architect. Not any old architect. Not even a good architect. But *the* architect; the architect of his age. A Nash of the twentieth century; a genius with impeccable taste.

Not that Robert fooled himself. He'd been a slow starter; despite all the application of which he was capable, he'd missed university by a whisker. So Bordfield Polytech and a steady slog to catch up with, and then overtake, the whiz-kids to whom it had once seemed so easy. He was doing it, too. One wall of his bedroom was bookshelf-lined, and every shelf was crammed with reading-matter covering the many and varied aspects of architecture. Far more than stresses and strains, designs and proportions. Social psychology was also part of the game; the subtle 'marking of territory' which, if done with cunning, built an invisible barrier against mindless vandalism; the stupidity – even unintentional cruelty – of "pigeon-hole" housing and tower blocks which slotted people side-by-side and above and below, but destroyed what had once been a community. 'Architecture is a damn sight more than telling some builder which bricks to use, and where to put the bogs. Done well, it makes for good living and good citizenship. Done badly, it makes for anarchy. Where a person lives determines what a person is.' The tutor, who barked that piece of priceless advice to an eager class, opened the doors of his chosen profession to Robert . . . and, from then on, there was no stopping him.

Therefore, and despite the domestic upheaval, Robert showed up at Bordfield Polytech and fought to push aside personal worries via study and work.

Nevertheless at morning break it showed. Friends – good friends who in the past had shared their laughter – glanced, then looked away. Steered an on-the-face-of-it haphazard course to another table in the canteen, and left him alone and lonely with his coke and his embarrassment. It wasn't deliberate cruelty. He wasn't being sent to Coventry. It was just that . . . *he was his father's son.* That simple. That uncomplicated. And given time – God only knew how much time – things would ease back to normal. Or would they? Because however long he lived he'd always be *that*: his father's son.

'Penny for them.'

The voice jerked him from his dark meditation. Sally had joined him and – although he kept the secret to himself – Sally was a very special person.

'You shouldn't be here.' The words, and the accompanying smile, carried bitterness.

'Why not?'

'The Copycat Ripper.' There was a split-second's pause, then he added, 'I might be dangerous.'

'Of all the stupid things to say!' The anger was genuine

39

enough. It was reflected in the savagery with which she ripped away the ring of the coke can. 'You ought to be ashamed of yourself.'

'Look around you, Sal.' And now there was a hint of apology and more than a hint of self-pity in the tone. 'I have leprosy ... something.'

She'd tipped the can to her mouth and now, having swallowed, she held the can, but with her forefinger pointing accusingly.

'Robert Drever, you are rapidly becoming a pain in the arse.'

'Look at them.' His voice rose slightly.

'I don't *have* to look at them. I know. They're sorry for you, but they're scared stupid of saying the wrong thing. Wouldn't *you* be?'

'I ...' He swallowed. 'I suppose.'

The can travelled to and from her mouth again, then she said, 'Y'know what? My old man was once done for Drunk in Charge. Stoned out of his crust he was. He could have killed anything. Anybody. Some innocent kid ... anything. It earned him six months and his job. Not *so* many years ago.'

'I don't see what ...'

'They let me drive my moped.'

'They?'

'The fuzz. The cops.'

'I still don't see ...'

'The same thing you poor, benighted idiot. My old man and me. Your old man and you. It's only a matter of degree.' She reached out and touched his hand with her fingers. There was a gentle quality in her voice as she bantered, 'Wooden legs, Robert. They don't run in families. Your dad's kinky about slags. *You're* kinky about cathedrals. Be grateful. Stay with cathedrals ... the most you can do is fall from a spire and break your stupid neck.'

Tears pricked the back of his eyes, but at the same time a shy smile twitched the corners of his mouth. This Sally – this one-off creature he was secretly crazy about – had a spellbinding quality all of her own.

In a more serious voice she said, 'Be patient with them, Robert. They like you. They're not giving you the cold shoulder ... honest. They like you. They *still* like you.'

'Yeah,' he gulped. He turned his hand and grasped her fingers. 'I – y'know – I like *you* . . . very much indeed.'

Anne busied herself about the house. Much of it was unnecessary; a Hoovering of what had already been Hoovered, a polishing of what was already polished. But something – anything – to keep the mind concentrated upon triviality and away from the subject which pulled like an electric magnet. At noon she made scrambled egg on toast; slowly and carefully and not, as was her usual manner, with a quick stir and a dumping of the mixture onto the slice as soon as it had popped from the toaster. The tea, too. The warming of the pot, the measuring out with apothecaric accuracy, the bringing of the pot to the kettle, the pouring the instant the water reached boiling point. Fiddling away the time. Filling each minute with sixty seconds of minutiae, in the hope that the concentration might form a wall of forgetfulness. It didn't. It merely formed a sieve, and the holes were greater than the strands. Liz was asleep upstairs. Liz was of paramount importance, therefore every fifteen minutes or so it was necessary to tip-toe into the bedroom to check that she was still asleep, and to re-arrange the beclothes in order that her nightgowned shoulders were protected from the October chill. Twice during the morning she'd telephoned the hospital. Each time the answer had been the same. 'She's progressing satisfactorily.' A stupid phrase. A meaningless phrase. 'Progressing'. A dying person 'progresses', but not in the right direction. And 'satisfactorily' could mean anything. Without pain. At an expected rate. Anything! In God's name, why couldn't the medical profession come down off its silly pedestal, and realise that people wanted to *know*? Or did they want to know? Did they really want to know, or did they really want an assurance? What if they'd said, 'She's dying. She's done what she wanted to do?' But they hadn't. They'd said, 'She's progressing satisfactorily.' Be thankful for small mercies. Be thankful for a vague answer upon which to hang hope.

And each time she'd passed the window – one of the windows – she'd seen the three waiting journalists. Waiting for what? The others had left; yesterday's news was today's history . . . so waiting for what? Just the three of them. One of them – a fat, Buddha-like creature – had stared unblinkingly back at her. An obese, vulture of a man waiting for the offal of whatever scandal he could root out. The other two were at least human; human enough to feel the cold, to stamp their feet, to flap their arms, to turn their head whenever they caught her eye. But the fat man was impervious to cold; standing there with his hands in the pockets of his shapeless, tent-like mac, his battered hat level atop his bloated face and out-staring her with bulbous, expressionless eyes.

It was a nightmare time and, because it *was* a nightmare time, it was peopled by creatures around whom nightmares could be woven.

It was also a very lonely time. Sitting there in the kitchen and away from the prying eyes of the fat man, she toyed with the scrambled egg on toast and felt lonely. Very lonely. Liz was asleep upstairs. Robert was at Bordfield. Mother was in Beech-wood Brook Cottage Hospital. Father was ... God only knew where father was. She was, it seemed, the only person left in the world. And it was a rotten world. A foul and cruel world, where decency counted for nothing and fat men could frighten you, merely by their presence.

She had to speak to somebody. Somebody! As she forked food into her mouth she decided to telephone Grandma and Gramp. When she'd eaten. She'd ring them. Talk to them. Tell them about the night's upheaval. They were nice people. They'd understand. They'd have sympathy, and the rift between them and Mother might be healed. It was worth a try. It wasn't fair that people who should be supporting each other at a time like this should be ...

As if her thoughts had in some way had an effect, the telephone bell began to ring.

In the main room she carried the telephone to a point where she couldn't be seen from the window; the last thing she wanted was the fat man staring at her as she held a private conversation. Then she lifted the receiver from its rest and held the mouthpiece closer to her lips than usual.

'Hello.'

'Anne? This is Babs.'

'Oh!'

Babs. Barbara Drever, her aunt and her father's sister. The line

42

crackled and hissed. It was to be expected; it wasn't a local call.

'I'm in the office. I'm coming up this evening.'

'Oh!'

Trust Babs. Trust Babs to arrive when the dust had settled . . . when she *thought* the dust had settled. Till now, she hadn't had time. 'Commitments, I'm afraid. You're in my thoughts – you're all in my thoughts – but I just can't make it. Darling, you sound worried.'

Why should I be worried? My father's just been convicted of multiple murder, my mother's just tried to commit suicide. What have I to be worried about? God, what sort of people did this aunt of hers consort with?

She forced herself to say, 'No. Not worried. Getting – y'know – getting used to things, I suppose.'

'Is Carol there?'

'No.' She swallowed, then added, 'She's out, I'm afraid.'

'Shopping, I suppose.'

Anne didn't answer the implied question, instead she said, 'What time will you arrive?'

'About nine. Probably nearer half-past. I can't get away till six.'

'But you can't possibly . . .'

'Worry not Anne, darling.' There was the silly teenage giggle, she mistook for a laugh. 'I'm coming up with a producer friend. He's travelling north on location. He has a Merc. The way he drives it makes the M1 look like a one-way street.'

Babs had lots of friends. All male. All with fast cars and always willing to oblige. No wonder she couldn't keep husbands; she'd had two already, and no doubt she'd already spotted a third potential.

'What's that Anne, darling?'

'Oh – er – nothing. Shall I ring and tell Grandma and Gramp?'

'Who? Oh, Bill and Mary . . . no, darling. Book me in for a couple of nights at a decent hotel. I'll call them when I arrive.'

'Bill' and 'Mary'. Great God, they were her *parents*! Old-fashioned parents and wonderful people. Their generation didn't go in for Christian names all round; age and a solid, respectable life earned a respect, and part of that respect was to be treated as parents by their own children.

Anne found herself saying, 'We've room for you here.'

'Look, darling, I don't want to barge in where . . .'

'You won't be barging in. There's plenty of room.'

'As I recall, you haven't . . .'

'Plenty of room, Aunt Barbara.'

'What?' The 'Aunt Barbara' had shaken her. Anne could visualise her staring, head-cocked, at the receiver.

'Plenty of room. No need to waste money on a hotel.'

Anne dropped the receiver onto its rest. She held it there as she took deep breaths in an attempt to control her rising anger. The stupid, conceited bitch. Didn't she realise how ridiculous she sounded? How ridiculous she looked? 'Babs' for heaven's sake. All right, it was 'Liz' and the relationship was the same. Exactly the same. But Liz had *earned* the right over the years. And Liz never put on airs, made believe she was something special, fooled around pretending to be younger than her years. Liz was . . . *Liz*. Whereas 'Babs' was Aunt Barbara being a pain in the neck.

On an impulse she removed her hand from the receiver and dialed a number.

Mary Drever entered the room from the tiny hall of the bungalow. 'Entered' rather than 'walked'. Her every movement was deliberate but slow; the knotting pain of rheumatoid arthritis killed any hope of hurry, and two years ago a moderately severe heart attack had brought her up with a jolt to the realisation that, in Biblical terms, her life span was on its last few laps. The G.P. hadn't minced words. 'You're not young any more, Mrs Drever. Slow down. Pace your life better. You can't pedal up hill as easily as you used to.' Nor had the advice needed any underlining; the stabbing agony at her joints was a constant reminder, and she was breathless without what she considered real cause. Some mornings she even awoke breathless, but that was something she kept from her husband. Nevertheless, her movements were slow and deliberate, even if her general carriage remained proud.

Bill Drever lowered the *Yorkshire Post* and said, 'Anne?'

'Yes.' She lowered herself gingerly into an armchair. 'Barbara's just called. She's coming up tonight.'

'Big of her,' grunted Drever.

'Anne says they'll put her up at their place.'

44

'Thank God for that.'

Bill Drever was Yorkshire; militantly Yorkshire. His un-spoken belief was that creation had merely learned its skills with the rest of the world; that the final, immaculate product had been the Broad Acre County. He was a retired builder. A 'jobbing builder' as he'd always insisted upon calling himself and, indeed, in almost half a century he'd only built half a dozen houses . . . plus the bungalow they now lived in. Not that his tiny workforce *couldn't* build houses; they could build better houses than most firms. But good workmanship and top class materials whittled away the profit margin, and it paid better to repair the crap less conscientious builders had been responsible for. What couldn't speak couldn't lie. Six houses and this bungalow in more than forty years, and not one of them had had to be 'repaired'; not so much as a loose slate or a blocked drain. Which was as it should be. A house was meant to last. If it was built right it *would* last . . . a damn sight longer than the men who built it.

As he raised his newspaper again Mary said, 'We'd best ask her over.'

'Why?' He lowered the newspaper and scowled.

'Bill!'

'Look, Mother.' He closed the newspaper, and eyed the only woman he'd ever looked at, much less kissed, with a gruff affection as genuine and as deep as it had been on the day of their wedding. 'She's not of our generation. How the hell her mind works is well beyond me.'

'Don't swear, Bill.'

Swear! By God, that had been one of the burdens of retire-ment. To mind his language. In the old days, back at the yard, he'd effed and blinded with the best whenever things had gone amiss. He'd had a tongue and he'd used it. But now . . .

'Sorry,' he apologised. 'But she's our daughter, and I've a right to speak my mind. She's doolally. You know it and I know it. That London crowd she's in with. They're all . . .'

'She's our lass, Bill.'

'Aye.' He took a deep, shuddering breath. 'Just like William's our lad. A bonny bloody pair, I must say.'

'Bill don't . . .'

'Dammit, I'll swear in my own house, Mother. What *he's* done

45

– what *she's* become – it's enough to make a saint swear.' His reading of the *Yorkshire Post* had occupied his mind, but now the anguish of the last few weeks, and especially of the last twenty-four hours, returned to furrow his face and sadden his eyes. There was terrible self-recrimination in his tone as he continued, 'We went wrong somewhere, lass. We didn't bring 'em up right. Dammit, what *did* we do, mother?'

'I don't know,' she said sadly.

'They had a good home. A good mother . . . none better.'

'Carol's cut her wrists,' she blurted out.

'Eh?'

'Cut her wrist. She's in hospital. Anne's just said.'

'How d'you mean "Cut her wrist"? What with?'

'Suicide,' she breathed. To her it was a near-forbidden word. Like swearing. 'She tried to commit suicide.'

'Oh, bloody hell!'

'Last night.' This time, despite his outburst, she didn't chide him. It was *his* way and he had cause. 'She's in hospital. Unconscious. Liz has been with her all night. Anne's on her own.

'What they'd do without Liz,' he sighed.

'I know.'

'Robert?'

'He's at college. He wanted to go. It seemed best.'

'Liz still with Carol?'

'No. She's in bed. She's jiggered.'

'I'll bet.' He folded the *Yorkshire Post* very carefully. It was his only reading matter; the only newspaper he believed. That and the BBC News. Everything else was suspect. In a heavy voice he said, 'We'd best get across there.'

'I'd hoped you'd say that.' She smiled a quick but sad smile of gratification. 'I'll make a bite. Save Anne the trouble.'

'Aye.'

With the same care and deliberation, she made her way into the kitchen. Her movements were slow but not wasteful; via trial and error she'd taught herself to remain an efficient housewife, despite her disability. She wouldn't have known the meaning of the expression "Time and Motion", but that's what it boiled down to. A place for everything, and everything within easy reach. That her husband didn't help meant nothing. He wasn't *expected* to help. The kitchen was her domain; a woman's work and beyond the limited capabilities of a man. He'd be in the way; he wouldn't know where things were; he'd be a hindrance rather than a help.

And as she worked, she remembered. So many things. About her daughter. About her son.

Bill had wanted him to work at the yard. To take over when his father retired. Natural; it was a good business and thriving; Bill had worked all hours to make a name. It was natural he'd wanted his lad to take over. But William wasn't Bill. Never had been. Like that never-to-be-forgotten time Bill had sent him up the ladder.

It was the old house; the house they'd lived in all Bill's working life; the house alongside the yard. A great, tall, rambling place. Three storeys. And cellars; one of the cellars was used as the plumber's workshop. On the ground floor one of the rooms was used as the office. Attics. Bedrooms, some of which they never used. And because Bill was Bill, it was kept in good repair. And it needed painting. Well, actually, it didn't *need* painting – it could have gone another two years and no harm done – but Bill said it needed painting, so it needed painting.

'William can help. Keep him out of mischief.'

It was the long summer holiday and William was only thirteen, coming on fourteen and, true enough, after the first two weeks he was tending to become a little bored.

'Start at the top. William can get the old stuff off, then sand-paper it down for priming.'

'It's a bit high, luv.'

'Eh?'

'High. He's only a bairn, remember.'

'He's old enough, mother. He has to learn. And the ladder's safe. *I'll* rope it into position. Don't worry.

And the pallor of the boy's face as he stared up the length of ladder. And the hint of a tremble on the lower lip.

'Now, just take your time, son. Shove one leg through a rung, you've watched 'em oft enough. You're safe. Nowt to worry about. Forget where you are. Concentrate on what you're doing.'

'Father, I think ...'

'Just take it easy. Don't rush. Blowlamp in one hand, scraper in the other. Make sure you burn the paint, not the wood. As soon as it starts blistering, that's enough. Scrape it off while it's still soft. You'll get the hang in no time.'

The slow, terrified climb.

'Don't hug the ladder, lad. Like you're walking upstairs, that's all.'

The slow – oh, so slow – threading of a leg between the rungs.

'That's it son. You're doing grand.'

'Bill, tell him to come down. He's terrified.'

'He's all right, mother. He *can't* fall now . . . even if he wanted to.'

'He can, y'know, Gaffer.'

'Eh?'

Jim. Jim Wells. Unskilled, only a labourer, but in a funny sort of way more understanding than any of the others. Quieter. No shouting and swearing. She watched him, sometimes, when he was working in the yard. At snack time he sat just a little bit apart from the others and, where they read the back pages of newspapers, Jim Wells read a book. Sometimes a library book. Sometimes a paperback.

'I'd get him down if I was you, Gaffer.

'Don't you reckon to be dry-mixing concrete, Wells?'

'Yes.'

'Then what the hell are you doing . . . Watch that blowlamp, lad. *Watch that flame! You'll have the bloody house alight*!'

'Bill, for God's sake . . .'

'Throw the blowlamp clear, William. Throw it well clear.'

'Wells. Who the hell . . .'

Then the blowlamp coming down and landed on the tarmac drive. An old-fashioned, petrol blowlamp. The burst; like a bomb exploding. The cloud of flame and smoke, and Jim Wells racing for the cement bags alongside the dry mix he was working at, and carrying an unopened bag, and smashing it down onto the flames. A hundredweight of cement, but it killed the fire.

Then climbing the ladder. Fast but gently, like a cat, trying not to make the ladder sway any more than possible. And the descent. Slowly. Carefully. Rung at a time. With Jim's head level with William's shoulders, and his strong arms forming a barrier, right and left, like the bars of a cage.

'I think you'd better take him into the house now, Mrs Drever. A nice hot drink and a lie down.'

'Thanks, Jim.' An unsuccessful search for the right words, and a final choked, 'Thanks.'

'Wells.'

'Yes, Gaffer.'

'When you've finished today call in at the office. Your cards'll be waiting.'

And the wry, soft-spoken, 'Yes, Gaffer,' but without bitterness and without surprise.

She wondered what had happened to Jim Wells. She'd often wondered. He'd deserved better, but he hadn't *expected* better. Bill had been a hard man in those days. Oh, aye, he'd softened a bit with age, but in *those* days . . . none harder.

They ate paté sandwiches and drank tea, the way Bill liked his tea, from half-pint beakers. And they talked, and their talk merely reflected their mystification. Suicide – attempted suicide – was beyond the stretch of their comprehension. In fairness so, too, was murder. And, on a lower level, the chosen life style of their daughter.

Theirs was a simple, uncomplicated world. A man grafted and earned every penny he handled. He took a woman as wife and she too knew her place in the scheme of things. She could cook, she could do a bit of sewing, she could take the weekly wash in her stride, she could keep a clean house and she could bring up kids. For that he paid her 'housekeeping' and wasn't mean, and he paid all the main bills – gas, electricity, rates, coal, much of the cost of clothes, other than underclothes – and if she could save a bit out of the 'housekeeping' it was hers to spend on what luxuries she fancied. But nothing daft till the family had been fed and the necessities had been paid for. She also kept herself decent; she remembered she was a married woman and acted accordingly. He in turn did the same; not too much booze and no spare women in the background. She didn't ask questions; she accepted that he knew his business and wasn't nosey about money matters. Often she didn't know, or want to know, how much he earned. On the other hand if he'd any pride, *he* didn't throw his money away; he saved, because he knew there'd come a day when he couldn't work – age or infirmity had to come sooner or later – and, God willing, she'd still be his wife and he'd still have to provide; live off the fat; live off the interest paid by some building society.

A simple, uncomplicated world; a world in which charity (neither the giving nor the receiving) had little place. Not a sharing, but rather a strict division of responsibility, understood and accepted . . . and it worked. It had worked well, and why in God's name it hadn't been held to by their two children neither could understand.

Bill Drever swallowed, washed his mouth with tea, and muttered, 'He needn't have thieved. Dammit he'd a good wage . . . he needn't have thieved.'

'He needn't have murdered,' said Mary sadly.

'No.' Drever scowled then, as if propounding some well-thought-out conclusion, added, 'Mind . . . I've felt like swinging for folk at times.'

'But them . . . *women.*'

'That's beyond me.'

'And – y'know – what he *did*. Not just killing them.'

'Anybody else . . .' The words rode on a heavy sigh. They meant nothing.

It was the way they talked; a form of communication they'd grown used to over the years. To an educated stranger – to anybody versed in the art of conversion – it would have been but one step beyond the grunts and mumbles of caveman speech. But *they* understood. To them it had meaning. To them it carried nuances beyond the pen of any poet.

Liz was up and about by early afternoon. She bathed, using Carol's bathroom because the scarlet stains on the other bathroom carpet had not yet been completely removed. She luxuriated in the hot, scented water and was of the opinion that she deserved no less.

Carol?

'Damn you, Carol,' she murmured quietly. 'Damn you for making a bad situation even worse.'

William?

Accept that William was weak. Accept that as long as she'd known him – for almost thirty years – she'd recognised him as a weak man. A man capable of being swayed and influenced by other people. An indecisive man. A man utterly incapable of making a promise and keeping it. Accept all this and yet ...

Murder is a very *decisive* act. Just about the most decisive act possible. Not a hot-blooded killing; not a towering rage, a sudden loss of control and something done in the seething heat of a maddened mind. No, not that. Something deliberate. Something planned. Something taken step by step, carried out and then embroidered on in order to make it even more diabolical. A *very* decisive act.

Therefore why William? What pressures were capable of driving a man like William to such extremes? To something so much out of character?

Of late – until he'd been arrested – he'd seemed his normal self. With hindsight perhaps a little more boisterous than he'd once been ... perhaps. Who could tell? A thing like this happens and you tend to examine the past day at a time – almost hour at a time – searching for pointers. Convinced there must have been *something*. Something you ought to have seen, but something you missed. A moodiness, perhaps. A dropped hint that you let slide by. Some tiny, unexplained episode. A slight change of mannerisms. Even a difference in the way he talked, the way he dressed, the way he responded to everyday situations. The mind was incapable of accepting the possibility that three murders, with accompanying sadistic foulness, produced no outward manifestations.

And yet with William ...

Oh, yes. Four years ago – *about* four years ago – but that was four years ago! A marital spat. Something and nothing. It had lasted a few weeks, and Carol had stormed around the house seething and finding fault. But husbands and wives carry on like that sometimes. And as far as possible – for the sake of Anne and Robert – they'd kept it to themselves, well almost.

'Liz don't *ever* get married.'

'It's not included in any plans for my immediate future.'

Looked at it from this distance, probably there had been a certain impassioned earnestness about her words. Probably. But on the other hand Carol had a habit of playing to the gallery.

'He's an animal. An absolute animal.'

'Oh, come *on*. He's not perfect, but ...'

'Don't argue, Liz. You're not married to him. You don't have to sleep with him.'

At which point good manners demanded that she ask no more questions and make no more observations. Pillow-talk and bedroom antics were sacrosanct; she was merely Liz, the obliging aunt and sister-in-law. But then two, maybe three, days later.

'Liz, I want to ask you something.'

'Yes.'

'You'll tell me the truth?'

'Of course.'

'Has he ever – y'know –' But the question had stuck in her throat.

'What?'

'Y'know. Made suggestions? *Done* anything?'

'Who? William?' And, after the initial shock, she'd almost laughed.

'You'd – you'd tell me?' And oh, the urgency in *that* question.

'Carol, that's an outrageous question. It's offensive.'

'You *would* tell me?'

'I wouldn't stay long enough to tell you. Anything – anything at all along those lines – and I wouldn't even wait to pack my bags.'

'No ... he wouldn't.' The frown of concentration. The absolute acceptance of the denial. 'No. Of course he wouldn't. Not with *you*.'

Strange how that last word had hurt. Stupid that it *should* have hurt. But Carol had a way of injecting words with very poisonous meanings. Okay she (Liz) was no breath-stopper; never had been, never made any pretence to be. But, God, she wasn't actually *ugly* ... not the way Carol had implied. Homely? Okay – homely – but that wasn't something to be sneezed at. She *could* have made a home. With the right man she could have made things work; that 'happy ever after' goal *could* have been reached. Kids, maybe. Maybe not ... who cared? With the right man it wouldn't have mattered too much. Just the two of them and, sure as hell, *he* wouldn't have gone to some hick town red light district and ...

52

Hold it, girl! Hold it right *there*.

Push that logic one inch farther – sit on that thought one second longer – and you're in very dangerous territory. Some excuses are not to be made. Are not even to be sought. *He's* the multiple murderer. *She's* only your sister. A very demanding sister, a not-too-loving sister, an occasional pain-in-the-fanny sister and *never* a 'sisterly' sister. But if that's a crime, that's the only crime she's committed, and she hasn't used a knife to commit it and, having committed it, she hasn't left three mutilated corpses . . . so, hold it, Elizabeth Stewart and let not your fancy go wandering along forbidden footpaths.

As if by cleansing her body she could equally cleanse her mind, she slid deeper into the water and made great play with the soap and the loofah.

The fat journalist was a professional to his fingertips. He frightened Anne, he was no shining example of man's ability to stand alongside the angels but, by Christ, he knew his job. He was the reason the two other journalists were there. Snout's nose for a story could have taken him to Fleet Street – to any of the big nationals – any day of any week. But unfortunately Snout's liking for strong liquor would on that same day of that same week have seen Snout back on a northbound train, with an editor's apologies to keep him warm.

But *The Bordfield and Lessford Star* fought an everlasting pincer movement with *The Northern Echo* and the *Yorkshire Post* and Snout was something the editor was willing to tolerate for the sake of circulation. Snout. It wasn't his real name, but it was the name he happily answered to. His by-line, whatever the story, was 'Our Own Correspondent' whether it appeared in *The Star* or whether he sold it to some other newspaper. Other than that, he was Snout. 'Snout, the old man wants you in his office.' 'Snout – line twenty-two – a call for you from Leeds. He wouldn't give his name.' Once upon a time – years ago – somebody had heard the features editor call him Gerald; one of the never-ending series of arguments concerning Snout's official status on the paper. A sort of plea for reasonableness. 'Gerald you're on *staff*. You can't go flogging pieces to all and sundry. This is a damn good number, we could have used it.' And he'd been talking to Snout, but because he was talking to Snout it had no effect. But other than on that one occasion he was Snout; the name he answered to and the name (nickname or surname) which fitted perfectly.

His two companions were younger men, slimmer men and, be it understood, men intimidated by Snout's reputation. They, too, were from *The Bordfield and Lessford Star*. One was a photographer. 'But keep that Box Brownie out of sight. I'll tell you when.' And when Snout rumbled instructions, lesser fry didn't argue. The third man was not far out of the cub-reporter stage; sent along to watch, learn, fetch and carry.

He it was who showed first signs of rebellion.

'Ask me, we're wasting our time.'

'Who asked you?' Snout's voice had been ruined by a combination of cheap booze, cheap cigarettes and standing for hours in lousy weather; it was a harsh gurgle, as if it had to be forced past a lamination of phlegm stuck in his throat.

'All the others have gone. It's been milked dry.'

'Laddie,' gurgled Snout, 'too many people leave the theatre before the punch-line. Drever's woman tried to do herself in last night.'

'Oh!'

The photographer said, 'You have that on good authority?'

'The Emergency Ward. She's still in.' Snout moved his head in a single nod as he kept his eyes fixed on the front windows. 'That house is a bomb, laddie. When it explodes I want pictures. I also want to be here to see it.'

'I – er – I didn't know,' said the young reporter apologetically.

'Such a lot, laddie,' sneered Snout. 'More than even *you* realise.'

Like one of those silly games with a wooden bat and a ball fastened to the centre of the bat with elastic; the ball flew away and the elastic stretched, then the ball whizzed back and either hit the bat with a bang or flew past and careered off in the opposite direction. A game without point or purpose. Just a flying ball you couldn't control. Coming at you, threatening to hit you, then flying past until it flew back and threatened to hit you again. A silly game. A frightening game.

'. . . take the drip off. Otherwise when they visit her . . .'

'. . . should have had something to quieten her before things got to . . .'

'. . . pitied rather than blamed. A cry for help, really. I doubt whether . . .'

'. . . when she comes round. It's not that she's ill. She's just . . .'

And the damp, rock-pocked sands of Whitsand Bay, and Liz and the kids racing and playing in the distance, well out of ear-shot.

'It's just that you don't even *try*.'

'Of course I try. I bend over backwards to be a good wife.'

And an expanse of sun-sparkling sea stretching beyond the reach of the eye. Rame Head, black and jutting in the distance. The wood-framed bungalows scattered, like multi-coloured sweetmeats on the green steepness leading from the beach.

'You're to be pitied. Y'know that? Self-grandeur. That's all you have going for you. A little man in big britches.'

'Jones doesn't think so.'

'Jones doesn't *know* you.'

'Well enough to offer me a directorship.'

'Of what? Some tin-pot firm on its last legs. My God, you aren't even a *chartered* accountant. You can add figures without making too many mistakes. They're putting you on and you're too blind to see it. You're dim . . . so dim you won't even know if they cook the books.'

'. . . coming round, doctor.'

'Is she? Ah . . . good.'

And the ball returned, faster than ever. Then the bat vanished and with it the ball and the elastic, and she opened her eyes and stared up at Bryant and a uniformed nurse.

'Where . . .' she breathed.

'You,' said Bryant with mock solemnity, 'have been a very stupid young lady. You've had us all very worried.'

With consciousness, memory returned and tears spilled from the corners of her eyes. A tiny stab of pain, almost too tiny to be noticed, accompanied the removal of the drip tube, and the nurse wheeled the stand towards the door of the ward.

'Have a good cry.' Bryant used a forefinger to ease a lock of her sweat-matted hair from one eyebrow. 'It's what you need, lassie.

What every woman needs now and again. Better than any tonic. Then when it's over, dry your eyes, blow your nose and press the bell-push.' He nodded towards the pear-shaped plastic above her head. 'We'll feed you then tidy you up for visitors.'

'I'm – I'm sorry,' she choked. Her hands were on top of the covers. She raised them, and stared at the bandaged wrist. 'I'm *so* sorry.'

'We all do daft things,' murmured Bryant. Then in a brisker tone. 'What would you like to eat? Toast? Toast and honey? I can recommend the honey. It's from a local bee-keeper. It's very good. Barbara Cartland would do handstands.'

She nodded and bit hard on her lower lip.

'And no more self-pity?'

Still biting her lower lip, she shook her head. She still wanted to cry, but it wasn't quite the same. Not heartbreak. Shame, but a peculiarly innocent shame; not the shame of identification with murder, mutilation and theft. Like a little girl being confronted by a beloved and slightly disappointed headmistress. Or in this case a head*master*. Not a doctor. Or if a doctor far *more* than a doctor.

Bryant smiled and played his part to perfection. He touched her bandaged wrist very gently as he spoke.

'No more of this nonsense.'

'N-no,' she promised, shyly.

'Eat you food, take your pills . . . and smile.'

She dutifully smiled. An ingenuous, quick upturning of the lips. Bashful. Coy. A compliment to the still-trickling tears.

Bryant grunted approval. He was a wise old bird and no mean actor. For the moment priority demanded the quietening of a mental storm. He didn't believe in fancy drugs when a deliberate 'bedside manner' could do the trick more cheaply and with fewer side-effects.

Robert Drever packed his books into a zip-topped plastic holdall with the words 'British Airways' stencilled in white across a blue background. He packed them carefully; even more carefully than usual, because he wanted to allow his fellow students time to vacate the lecture room before he left. It may have been his imagination but they in turn seemed to be more than usually anxious to leave. He sighed, because it *may* have been his imagination, and if it was, that was one more factor he must learn to watch.

He walked slowly along the corridors and out into the chill and wet October afternoon. He took the shallow steps one at a time, kept his head lowered as if against the weather, and looked neither right nor left.

Sally Oldfield was waiting for him. She was standing on the squelchy grass, alongside the path leading from the steps, and she moved out to walk alongside him as he made his way towards the gates. For almost twenty yards neither of them spoke. Indeed, to a casual observer, Robert seemed unaware of her presence. But she knew better, and she it was who broke the awkward silence.

'Burger?' she suggested gently.

Without looking up he muttered, 'You'll be late home. They'll worry.'

'They won't worry,' she contradicted.

'You'll have a meal waiting.'

'One burger won't ruin my appetite.'

'Sal . . .' He closed his lips on whatever argument he was going to make, moved his shoulders and grunted, 'Okay.'

Sal (he knew) was ploughing her way through one of the 'sociology' courses . . . and 'ploughing' was the right word. She found it hard going because she refused to accept the broad generalities so beloved of pseudo-experts whose arrogance insisted that they understood all mankind. 'Such crap! You can't shove a few million people into one cage and label 'em like so many monkeys.' He knew she wouldn't make it. She was too much of a rebel. He doubted whether she'd even finish the course. But he hoped she would, because she had her eyes on the Probation Service and, from what he'd heard, that service needed as many people like Sal as possible . . . and anyway if she ducked out she'd leave the college, and that meant she'd leave *him*.

The small-time entrepreneur had his finger on the likes and dislikes of the student generation. The Formica-topped tables were cunningly positioned; party or *tête-à-tête* were equally catered for. Canned music came from high speakers; loud

57

enough to hear, but not loud enough to interfere; modern stuff, but not *too* way-out, with a smattering of Jacques Loussier and Dave Brubeck for the less with it customers. The buzz of talk was punctuated and paragraphed by shouts to and from the kitchen and, like a gentle sea mist, the faint smell of frying onions filtered through from the rings and grills. They ordered beefburgers and frothy coffee and having paid they threaded their way to a quiet corner, sat opposite each other and, in effect, dismissed the rest of the world from the earth.

'You're taking it hard, Rob.'

It was nice the way she called him 'Rob'. Not 'Bob' like all the other students. Not 'Robert' like the family. 'Rob' was her name for him, and he might have been mildly offended had anybody else shared it.

'It's ... difficult,' he admitted cautiously.

'It's all over.'

'No.' He shook his head, sadly. 'That's how it happens in newspapers. In books. In real life ... no way. It's *never* over.' He stirred the coffee slowly. Opened his heart to somebody for the first time. 'Think about it Sal. Some interview for a job. *Every* interview. "Drever? Haven't I heard that name before somewhere? Some maniac who killed three women?".' He paused and stared at the surface of the coffee. 'It's not a common name, Sal. They'll remember. They'll ask.'

There was both truth and exaggeration in his thinking, but while there was truth, the exaggeration counted for nothing. To make other than sympathetic noises would have been foolish.

She bit into her beefburger and watched his face across the table. For an eighteen-year-old it seemed a very mature face; not quite the face of Rodin's *Thinker*, but with the same solemn concern about important things.

She tasted coffee then, matching solemnity with solemnity, she said, 'You're a nice guy, Rob. You'd make a smashing fella.'

He looked startled. The implication of her words didn't immediately communicate itself.

She elaborated, 'One day some bird's gonna be very lucky.'

'I – er – y-you?' It was a stammered, whispered plea.

'I'm talking about something serious, Rob.'

'I-I know.'

'Not just good friends. A good time. Doing things for laughs.'

'Would you?' he breathed. 'Please?'

'You *mean* it?' And now she was a little breathless.

'God! Do I *mean* it?'

She lifted one of her fingers – the forefinger of her right hand – raised it to her mouth and touched it with her lips. Then she leaned forward slightly and touched his lips with the same forefinger. It was a gesture – a very sombre and once-and-forever gesture – and, although the finger carried the hint of grilled beefburger, that was okay. It was 'their' taste. 'Their' smell. And over the speakers Brubeck's *Take Five* hiccuped its catchy five-four-beat melody and, as from that moment, that became 'their' tune.

Whoring. The so-called 'oldest profession in the world'. Certainly one of the most dangerous professions. One of the most misunderstood professions. 'Hell, a whore can't have any real emotion – a whore can't love or have any *real* feelings – look what she does for a living.' Never the man, always the whore. A man screws around like crazy, and earns himself the name of 'a bit of a lad'. But every woman who helps him along the road to that reputation loses her own and is tabulated as 'a slag'.

But so often a woman sells her body because it is the only saleable commodity she possesses; she has no clerical skills, her education – albeit at times the education imparted at some expensive but totally inadequate school – is well below par and she is left with a straight choice. Marriage or whoredom. And with the wrong man marriage *is* a form of whoredom, and badly paid at that.

She makes a choice. She trades in lust – she does *not* trade in love – and, unlike so many of her 'respectable' sisters, she knows that lust and love are two eternal incompatibles. Like Janus, the act of sex has two faces. One cheap although at times expensive. The other priceless. Therefore, because her profession demands that she spend much of her life staring into the dark face, she treasures the occasional glimpse of the brighter face all the more. The apparent contradiction then; the logic which remains unacceptable to the narrow-minded. The true whore knows all about love – *real* love – and values it at its true price.

Ruth Linley knew the truth of all this. As 'Red Ruth' she'd

once traded herself without deception. She'd charged high and given good value; she'd filled out her Income Tax returns with scrupulous honesty; she'd scorned the use of pimps or protectors; she'd saved and invested . . . and now she'd retired. She was probably the most honest person within her own circle of friends and, be it understood, that circle included men *and women* of some standing in the community. By normal standards she was a wealthy woman, and although the original source of her wealth was fairly common knowledge, her self-taught taste more than counter-balanced her one-time mode of life. She'd retired. She'd closed a door, very firmly, and what she'd once sold was not available as a sop to temporarily irate husbands. That fact, too, was known. It was appreciated by the married ladies who were not ashamed to call her their friend.

And yet, she'd known love. The love of a man – one man – and the love of a child.

'Darling, I'm in no position to raise objections worth a damn. But I can give advice. Have rules and stick by them. Know how far you're prepared to go. Know what money *can't* buy. And build a wall around yourself, darling. A very thick, very high wall. And let nobody inside that wall unless you're sure . . . and I mean *sure*.'

She remembered that conversation, almost word for word. It had happened a long time ago, but it was one of those conversations which mark milestones in everybody's life. Experience dragging the anchor on enthusiasm. In restrospect, that's what it sounded like. Could be every piece of parental advice in history had had that same ring. Maybe Emma Hamilton's old lady had made similar noises.

She pulled the Triumph Alpine into the kerb and braked. Leaning sideways, across the front passenger seat, she attracted the attention of a passing police constable. She asked for directions and, having given them, the constable touched his helmet in a half-salute. And why not? A nice lady. A very polite, very respectable lady. A pity there weren't a lot more of her kind – a lot fewer mouthy tarts – around.

Bill and Mary Drever were more relaxed than they'd been the previous evening. The final shock – the shock of the verdict and the sentence, plus the shock of learning about William's thieving – had worn off. The shock, but not the knowledge and not the shame. But (as they were learning) knowledge and shame can be handled; involved and tortuous excuses can be made; inconvenient truths can be elbowed aside and ignored.

On top of which, Carol wasn't around.

'Where's Robert?' asked Bill Drever.

'He isn't home yet.'

Anne fussed around her grandparents. Last night's memory had to be buried beneath a fluffing of cushions and a positioning of footstools and ash-trays. Gramp had to be encouraged to smoke a pipe; doctor's orders had made him cut down a lot, and the dark shag he favoured *had* a foul and pervading smell, but no matter. Mother wasn't around to complain.

'A snack, Grandma?'

'No, luv. Thanks, but we had something before we left.'

Bill Drever packed the bowl of his pipe. Slowly and with a sense of anticipation. Bloody doctors! All this anti-smoking talk. In the old days people smoked; never a pipe or a Woodbine out of their mouths. They lived. They coughed a bit – cleared their tubes – but it didn't mean owt. They lived. Some of 'em lived to a ripe old age. Bit o' baccy didn't see 'em off. Good God, a man was entitled to *one* vice. If it stopped at smoking, no harm done.

In a slightly awkward voice he asked, 'How's your mother?'

'When I left she was asleep. They'd given her drugs.'

Liz answered the question. She was up and dressed. A little pale, a little tired-eyed, but otherwise her usual smart and efficient self.

'I'm going in to see her later,' added Liz.

'You go?' Anne made the question a gentle plea.

'Nay.' Bill Drever snapped the fasteners of the pouch. 'I don't like them places.'

'She'll understand,' added his wife.

Oh, yes, she'll understand. She's *always* understood. Since before she married William she's understood. Your precious son was too good for her . . . your opinion, not his. Even now – despite what he's done – he's still too good for her. What *he's* done is nothing compared with what *she's* done.

61

'What in God's name made her do it?' Bill Drever almost seemed to have read Liz's thoughts.

'The accumulation, I suppose,' fenced Liz.

Mary Drever said, 'She's not alone, you know.'

'She's his wife.'

And she *is* alone. You may not think so, *I* may not think so, but while *she* believes herself to be alone, she's alone. So, if you're so sure she's not alone, why not visit her? Why not *show* her? Why not at least make an attempt at compassion?

'Aunt Babs is coming ... I told you,' said Anne hurriedly.

Liz added, 'She can sleep here.' Then, almost spitefully, 'She can have Carol's room.'

'Will she like that?'

'Babs or Carol?'

'Does it matter a damn?' Bill Drever held the match ready to strike it on the side of the box. 'Does it really matter a damn?'

'Bill!'

'No, dammit, I'll have my say. This house. Who does it belong to? Who owns it? When it comes to stick and lift, who the hell *says* who sleeps where?'

'That's not the point. It's ...'

'That *is* the point, mother. A man gets married – never mind who he gets married to – a man gets married, he accepts responsibilities. Dammit, if he doesn't do that he's no business getting married. He provides a home – a house – he doesn't let somebody buy the damn thing from under him. He's a wife and kids. He *remembers* that. God Almighty, they have to *live* somewhere, it's not that bloody difficult.'

'Your son,' Liz reminded him gently.

'Aye, lass. My son.' The fury eased and reluctant affection was there as he gazed at her. He continued looking at her as he lighted the tobacco, looking at her through the smoke, and speaking between each draw he made. 'My son. My daughter.' He seemed to be accepting full and sole responsibility for what they were. 'A bonny bloody pair. Him ... well, never mind. But she's as bad. Husbands. She collects 'em like some folk collect stamps. Where the hell did they get it all from? Not from us. That I swear ... not from us. I don't give a damn where she sleeps. She can sleep in the gutter for all I care. Happen that's where she belongs.'

'Bill, you shouldn't . . .'

'Mother!' He waved out the match, then dropped it into the ash-tray. 'Who the hell do they think about? Who the hell do they *care* about? Either of 'em. Not us. They're above us, they've left us. Dammit, it wasn't *us* she telephoned. Carol. That's who she telephoned. Carol and her. About on a par, I'd say.'

It was the final condemnation of his daughter; that she was 'on a par' with the woman his son had married.

Ann burst out, 'Gramp, that's unfair.'

'Don't argue with your grandfather, pet.'

'But, Grandma, it's not . . .'

'Why shouldn't she argue with her grandfather?' Liz seemed to push aside her obvious tiredness. She stepped forward, as if to shield Anne from the bigotry of the older couple. 'Why shouldn't she defend her mother?'

'You're her mother's sister. Naturally you're . . .'

'Naturally nothing! I'm neither condemning nor accusing. There's been too much of that already.'

'Liz, lass.' Bill Drever moved his pipe in a tiny wave of silence as his wife made as if to speak. 'Nobody's blaming you, Liz. Nobody's blaming Anne, nobody's blaming Robert. But *somebody's* to blame. I don't know who. That's all I'm saying. Somebody.'

'Not Babs, surely?' The lips curled a little. The eyes glinted. 'Because she's "different"? Chose to be "different"? Can't make Yorkshire pudding, perhaps? Can't make parkin? Doesn't "thee" and "thou" it every time she opens her mouth? Or is that too one of the reasons? One of the reasons for William?' She closed her mouth into a tight line, as if to stop the outburst before it went too far. She took a deep breath then in a quieter voice said, 'Grandfather Drever. Grandmother. You're hurt. We're all hurt. But that includes Anne and Robert. For God's sake, leave them their mother. Don't try to make them emotional orphans.'

The Triumph Alpine parked opposite the gate and as the woman climbed out and locked the car door the fat newspaperman's bulging eyes grew greedy.

'The fuse,' he croaked. 'The detonator.'

'Eh?' The young reporter glanced at the woman, then back at

63

the fat man.

'Remember what I said about an explosion, laddie?'

'Oh!'

The woman walked across the darkening street. A steady walk. Firm and self-confident, but without brashness. The walk complemented the clothes, the hair-style, everything. The young reporter watched her, and words like 'lady' and 'gentlewoman' touched his mind.

As she drew abreast of them the fat man rumbled. 'Ruth.'

'Snout.' She smiled recognition, but her step neither slowed nor faltered. 'Ever the ubiquitous Snout. Always where he should be.'

Snout chuckled. A gurgling, disgusting sound.

Liz answered the ring.

'Mrs Drever – Mrs Carol Drever – is she at home?'

'No she's ... I'm afraid she's not at home.' Liz eyed this distinguished-looking woman with the suspicion of people recently subjected to unwanted publicity.

'When will she be back?'

'Not for some days.'

'I see.' The woman smiled. 'You're – let me see – you're Elizabeth Stewart, am I right? Newspaper photographs. Mrs Drever's unmarried sister.'

'Yes.' Liz's face darkened. 'Are you from some newspaper? Some ...'

'No.' The smile remained. A friendly enough smile and not at all intimidating. 'My name's Ruth Linley ... the mother of one of the murdered girls.'

Good families are generally worse
than any others.

The Prisoner of Zenda
Anthony Hope

From beyond the closed door came the sounds of a stretcher-trolley being wheeled along the corridor. The wheels needed oiling and the rhythmic squeak didn't quite dovetail in with the gentle slap of plimsol soles on the parquet floor. The matron's office smelled of flowers; an autumn smell, originating from the large vase of yellow and bronze chrysanthemums standing on the tiny side-table. One part of Liz's mind thought the flowers should be in one of the wards where they might be appreciated more, but on the other hand perhaps they were a very personal gift. It was reasonable to assume that even hospital matrons had admirers; that away from their charges and out of uniform they were as feminine as the rest.

'Not angry at all?'

'No . . . not at all angry.'

'She could have been hiding it.'

'It's possible. *Just* possible. But I doubt it.'

Bryant rubbed the back of his neck ruminatively. It disturbed the grey hair and gave his tonsured-like skull an oddly untidy but attractive appearance. An absent-minded-professor look.

'Who do you say was there?' The question was unnecessary, but it bought him time for consideration.

'Carol's parents. Anne, her daughter. And me of course.'

'And you didn't tell them?'

'No. I made some excuse about newspaper people.'

'Wise. Very wise.'

'Should I mention it to Carol?' asked Liz. 'That's my problem. A hint, perhaps?'

'No hint.' Bryant was quite firm. 'For the moment just make sympathetic noises. Meanwhile . . .'

He stopped rubbing his neck and instead began to tweak at an ear-lobe. The impression was of mild nervous agitation. The old smoothie, who'd turned on the paternal charm in the presence of the younger sister, seemed strangely ill at ease. For her part Liz had taken pains with her appearance; lipstick used sparingly but with care; her hair well brushed and combed and with a minimum of spray; something of a decision, when it came to a choice of clothes.

Nor had she pressed Anne too hard.

'I think you should go.'

67

'No.'

'Your mother will be disappointed.'

'Somebody has to stay with Gran and Gramp. Anyway Robert isn't home yet. He'll want a meal.'

'If you're sure.'

'Sure I'm sure. I'll visit tomorrow . . . if she's still there.'

And Mary Drever had added, 'Carol won't want a young army milling around her bed.'

Well a sister and a daughter didn't add up to a 'young army' and Bill and Mary had obviously no intention of hospital hopping, but Liz hadn't argued. Just that it was sad. People! Even decent, good-living people who, had you asked, would have counted themselves blessed with their full share of compassion. Even family. My God, these were rough times for the family; times when members supposedly moved in close and formed a wall against intruders. That's what the book of rules said . . . assuming there *was* a book of rules. But maybe there wasn't. Maybe some crappy script writer had invented the rule book as a basis for meaningless dialogue mouthed by tired actors and actresses in a fourth-rate movie. Maybe families – all families – turned a little sour when a real louse crawled out of their personal woodwork.

Even herself . . .

Don't give yourself airs, girl. Forty-five summers behind you and you've ponced yourself up just a *leetle* bit, on the off-chance that this medic might be around. Nothing to be too proud of eh? Not the recognised priority with a sister who's tried to commit suicide and a brother-in-law who's just heard the prison door slam because of his excursion into the realms of wholesale carnage. Not the 'done' thing . . . quite.

Bryant murmured, 'She'll be ready to see you.'

'What? Oh! Yes.' She angled around for things to say in order to prolong the stay in the matron's office. 'About this Linley woman?'

'Don't even mention her.'

'She's staying at *The Wounded Hart*.'

'Four star?' Bryant raised slightly surprised eyebrows.

'She's not – er – y'know . . .'

'Without? Obviously. How long is she staying?'

68

'Till she can talk with Carol.'

Bryant clicked his tongue.

'So . . . you see.' Liz moved her hands. 'She has to *be* told.'

'Not today.'

'Look . . .' The hands continued to move; fluttering, helpless movements. 'If *I* went to see her?'

'The Linley woman?'

'To see what she *really* wants?'

'You're taking a lot of unnecessary responsibility.' His hand left his ear, and he shoved both hands into the pockets of his trousers. He scowled at the surface of the desk. 'It just might be dangerous. Have you thought of that?'

'I don't see . . .'

'Put yourself in her shoes.'

'She didn't sound vindictive.'

'Your daughter's been murdered. Very savagely murdered.' He ignored her remark; spoke as if she hadn't said anything. 'The one thing you're not is a friend of the man responsible. Or a friend of his family. That's common sense. She *might* be planning to get her own back. That's not just a possibility. It's a *probability*.'

'You mean kill Carol?'

'No, not *kill* her. But something.'

Bryant wondered why the blazes *he* was concerned. Then, being an uncommonly honest man, he called himself an old fool for pretending not to know why he was concerned. The Drever woman was something of a pain in the neck; one of those creatures who treat medics as if they were quacks until it's too late, then expect all to be forgiven and everybody to run around in circles tending her fevered brow. She'd known – she *must* have known – she'd needed a quietener-down after her ordeal. *Must* have known. But oh, no! She was a tough baby. 'Cast Iron' Carol Drever, no doubt. That's who'd she'd thought she was. Something special. Something unique. Fine, so be it, but even cast iron cracks if it's subjected to too much pressure. And that left this Stewart lassie holding the can. A can not of her making, but . . .

He found himself murmuring, 'If I could be of help in any way.'

Liz looked puzzled.

'When . . .' Bryant flapped his elbows. 'If you intend visiting this Linley woman. Before you tell your sister.'

'I'm sorry, I don't . . .'

'I could go with you,' mumbled Bryant.

'Oh!'

'I don't want to push myself.' The words were still little more than a mumble. 'Just that . . .'

'*Would* you?'

'Of course, you may have somebody else in mind. Might have . . .'

'No. Nobody.'

'You need *somebody*.'

'I – I suppose so.'

'That's fixed then.'

'If – y'know – if you're quite sure it wouldn't be . . .'

'When?'

'Well, I – er – I was thinking I'd go straight from here. After I've had a chat with Carol. But if that's . . .'

'I'll be hanging around.'

'Thanks.' Liz swallowed. She was aware of the colour which was creeping up from her neck and flushing her face. 'Thank you very much. I – er – I won't stay longer than is strictly necessary.'

'Take your time.' Bryant pulled his hands from the pockets of his trousers, stepped across the office and held open the door. 'A few temperatures to take. A handful of prescriptions. I'll be waiting in the car.'

The last thing Anne wanted to do was hurt. The idea, when it was proposed, took her breath away. She knew the shock showed on her face, and she turned away, hopefully before they read the signs; hurried into the kitchen on the pretence of preparing a meal for Robert. In fact, to steady herself, and work out a way of refusing the offer without making Grandma and Gramp even more miserable.

'Anne, pet, how would you like to come and live with us?'

'You mean *forever*?'

'We'd look after you, pet.'

The idea, of course, was prepostperous. Like – like playing

Snap. Dealing the cards one at a time until the whole pack had been used up. Until there wasn't a pack left. But a family wasn't a pack of cards. You couldn't *do* that sort of thing to a family. Mother, Liz, Robert and herself were a *family*. They'd lost one member. That was all. Temporarily, they'd lost one member. That made them less complete, but they were still a family. Daddy wouldn't be away forever, then they'd be complete again. These last few days – these last few weeks – it had been awful, but they were still a *family*.

'Think about it, pet. There's no hurry.'

But she didn't *have* to think about it. What would happen to Mother? What would happen to Robert? What would happen to poor Liz? Liz would be left stranded. No! She – Anne – was the one person holding this family together. Without her they'd all fly off in different directions, and they'd be lost. They'd never get together again. They might never even *see* each other again.

And people said age brought experience. Brought wisdom. But it didn't ... did it? Grandma and Gramp. They were old. But they weren't wise. They couldn't even *see*. A thing so obvious, a thing that didn't even have to be explained, but they couldn't *see*.

And where the hell was Robert? She needed somebody. Needed somebody urgently. But Mother was in hospital, and Liz was visiting her, and the only person left was Robert. And he wouldn't come. Today of all days, he was late home.

'You could use Gramp's car to get to and from work.'

But I don't want your silly car. I don't even want *you*. No – that's wrong, that's wicked – I want you there in the background. Somewhere to visit. Somebody to fuss over. But not forever, and not all the time. I – I don't want to be there when you die. I'm sorry – truly sorry – but I don't want to be there to *watch*. I couldn't stand it. I'm not a nurse. I'm not even like Liz. I couldn't do it. I couldn't stand it.

The film of moisture made her vision blurred. Nor could her mind concentrate properly. What would Robert like? What would he like to drink? Tea, perhaps? Earl Grey? No, not Earl Grey. He'd recently made some muttered remark about 'scented tea'. Coffee then? Yes, she'd brew some instant coffee. Despite his 'scented tea' remark, his taste buds weren't *so* delicate.

Cheese and tomato sandwiches? Crusty bread with lashings of butter, and cheese and tomato, with a dollop of sweet pickle? That might be to his taste, she thought.

Liz would have known. Liz wouldn't have hesitated. And now they wanted to ...

She swung open the fridge door and the cool draught caught her face. Cool. Cold. Like death. Why had her life suddenly become concerned with death? The three murdered women. Mother trying to kill herself. And now her grandparents, and one of the reasons for not wanting to live with them ...

And why was Grandma so obviously anti-Liz? Anti-Liz and anti-Mother. But *why*?

'We'll take care of your mother, pet. And don't worry about Liz. Liz can look after herself.'

Well, of course she can. Look after herself, and look after Mother, and look after Robert, and look after *me*. And that's who we *want* to look after us. Without Liz Mother might have died. *Would* have died. Liz was pretty wonderful, when you stopped to think. She tended to be taken for granted, but shouldn't be taken for granted. Because between them – between herself and Liz – they could keep this family in one piece. They could talk Mother out of doing anything silly again. They could look after Robert, and help him become a great architect. They could make things *work*.

But if she left and went to live with Gramp and Grandma, it couldn't be done. Even Liz couldn't do it alone, therefore it wouldn't work, and the family would become a pack of cards being dealt out by people who didn't understand.

Sickness has a smell of its own. Nothing to do with drugs or medicines; nothing to do with antiseptics and soiled bandages; nothing to do with hospitals or even the home sickbed. Just sickness of itself. Be it disease, be it injury, be it merely some inconvenient ailment. The stench is there. A curious compound of incapacity and self-commiseration. And the side-ward stank of it.

'Feeling better?' Liz pulled a chair nearer to the bed and sat down. She nursed her handbag and gloves on her lap. 'The doctor says you'll be out in a couple of days.'

'Where's Anne?' said Carol weakly.

Some of the weakness was pure put-on. Of course she felt weak, but she also felt ashamed, and by emphasising one she tried to make less the other. Not deliberately, you understand. But the mind can make such decisions without conscious thought.

Liz said, 'Grandfather and Grandmother Drever came over. Anne's stayed at home to look after them.'

'Why?'

'Well, somebody had to ...'

'No, I mean why have *they* come over.'

'They're worried. We're all worried.'

'But not worried enough to visit me.'

'Carol, darling,' lied Liz, 'we didn't know. You might still have been under.'

The smile was weak and unconvinced. She wanted self-pity, and this was one more peg upon which to drape it. Liz leaned forward, and made play at fluffing out the pillows.

'Why didn't you let me finish it?' whispered Carol.

'That's a stupid question,' said Liz brusquely. She settled back on the chair. 'You happen to be my kid sister. You're also the mother of two fine children.'

'And the wife of a monster.'

Liz compressed her lips a little, but didn't comment.

Carol breathed, 'Why didn't you take him away from me?'

'What?' The frown was quite genuine.

'Way back. At the beginning. You were keen on him. You could have had him. Why didn't you?'

'That's silly talk.'

'Then you'd have been here, and I'd have been sitting in that chair making empty excuses.'

'I liked him. I've always liked him. I didn't love him.'

But the words were stilted and not quite true. She *had* liked him. Liked him a lot. Maybe it could have grown to be something else. Maybe it *was* something else, but something they both refused to let happen. You don't pinch your kid sister's man. Not if you've any sense of common decency. You don't go around ...

'I think he'd have dropped me like a hot brick.'

'He was besotted with you,' she said in a low voice. 'Nobody else had a look-in.'

'Lucky me.' The bloodless lips curled sardonically.

Besotted, was he? Not for long though. Perhaps until the kids were born, but after that there was a gradual change. 'Out with the boys'. She'd goaded him more than once.

'Out with the boys tonight? Out on a pub crawl?'

'Don't be so damn stupid. Clients – customers – some of them can't make the time during the day.'

'Clients'. 'Customers'. That's what he called them. After this little lot it didn't take much imagination to guess the truth. 'Clients' and 'Customers' all wearing black frilly underwear, no doubt. All tarts, grabbing at their slice of that seventy-thousand quid he couldn't afford.

She said, 'Thinking about it. Here alone – thinking about it – he's been a real sod. I'm glad they caught up with him.'

'Don't think about him,' said Liz curtly.

'Don't *you*?' she teased.

'I try not to. It's a very unproductive exercise.'

A nice phrase that. 'Unproductive exercise'. It rolled off the tongue very easily. Come to that, it summed up her whole life. A fancy way of saying she'd run around like crazy for the last forty-five years and ended up with damn-all. Substitute-mother to two marvellous kids, and substitute-mother to *their* mother. But always substitute. Never the real thing. She could, she supposed, have been substitute-wife. Had she played her cards right William had been hers for the plucking. Nothing obvious, of course. No fluttering eye-lashes. No come-to-the-bedroom glances. But more than once she'd seen him deflated to the point of near-madness. Carol had the knack. Give her something – somebody – she could drive the old knife into and she couldn't resist the temptation.

'My husband has a very limited stock of anecdotes. You must excuse him if he tends to repeat himself. He doesn't *mean* to bore you.'

That, and a few dozen similar remarks, each made with a saccharine smile and uttered with just the right amount of artificial gaiety. And she (Liz) had suffered for the poor devil. Squirmed with embarrassment for him. Been momentarily ashamed of this younger sister of hers. But done nothing and said nothing. Because they were man and wife, and if *he* was prepared to take it without retaliation, what real business was it of hers? But on those occasions – later when the guests had gone home and Carol had gone to bed and she (Liz) had trotted around the house collecting glasses and emptying ash-trays – there had been moments. But the moments had passed, and a new dawn had lightened the sky and, as always, it had ended up as an 'unproductive exercise'.

A nice phrase that. 'Unproductive exercise'. Her woozy mind wondered where Liz had picked it up. Very good. *Very* good. It just about summed everything up. The marriage, herself, the lot. Because, by God, she'd tried. Tried, but never succeeded. And okay she wasn't 'domesticated' ... never had been. Nobody had *taught* her. A simple thing – a very fundamental reason – he'd never fully grasped. The number of times, in the privacy of the bedroom, as she'd brushed her hair and as he'd padded around in pyjamas and dressing-gown.

'William, there's something wrong. I'm going *wrong* somewhere.'

'Who says?'

'You don't *have* to say. I can see it in your eyes. I'm not what you expected me to be.'

'You're my wife.'

'I carry your name. I've given you two kids. But that's *all*.'

'You're tired. You're not thinking straight. Leave it.'

'I'm *not* tired.'

'No? That makes a bloody change.'

Thus the bickering. The same things said over and over again in different words. The hurt piled upon hurt until all feeling was gone. The numbness. The marriage that was far more than a failure. It wasn't even a friendship ... and all because he wouldn't sit down and talk things out. An 'unproductive exercise' masquerading as a man-and-wife act.

Liz said, 'Babs is coming up later this evening.'

'What are we going to do, Liz?' That was how interested she was in William's sister. 'Without the house, without a home. What are we going to do?'

'There's the Cornish place.'

'There'll still be bills to pay. We can't live on *nothing*.'

'It's holiday country.' Liz made a quick, resigned mouse. 'We

75

could set something of a stall up. Cream teas. That sort of thing.'

'Oh, that *would* be nice. Frilly aprons and fairy cakes. That would be *really* nice.'

'You asked.' There was a snappish quality about the words.

'We might be able to use William – what he's done – as some sort of gimmick.'

'I think I'll go.' She made to rise from the chair. 'You're still feeling too sorry for yourself to see straight. I'll . . .'

'No! Please.' And now the tears weren't far away. Like a seesaw – like a switchback – either heartbroken or bitchy. Why, in hell's name, couldn't she be normal. She choked. 'It's me, Liz. I'm sorry. I've – I've taken more than I can stand. That easy. But I'll try. Truly. I'll try to be good. Guide me. Help me, Liz. For God's sake, help me. If – if *you* don't . . .'

Sal Oldfied was an only child, but an only child with a difference. She was loved, but not spoiled. Her father, David Oldfield, worked in the Trustee Department of one of the big four high street banks, and knew both the value and the worthlessness of money; he had seen friendships and families smashed for the sake of a few paltry thousand and, because of this, he recognised money as a necessity, but refused to acknowledge it as a god. Her stepmother was everything a stepmother should not be according to the fairy stories. She was gloriously untidy and monumentally unforgetful; there was a chaotic virtuosity in the way she allowed everything to be in its wrong place, and she spent hours writing out lists of things she had to buy, but forgot to take a list with her when she went shopping. Thus the house was in a perpetual state of shambles and near-panic, but every space was crammed with the sort of love a seventeen-year-old can appreciate.

Three years ago, when she'd married David, she'd taken a slightly apprehensive stepdaughter aside and, very solemnly, put things onto a firm basis.

'Sal, I'm not your mother. That's a slot I can never fill, and I'd be a fool if I tried. All I am is a woman, crazy about your father, and wanting to make his life a little happier. To do that I need your help. Without your help I can't do it. But, between us, we just might be able to ease the hurt. Not make him forget her . . .

that would be wicked. Just make the memory a little less painful. What say, Sal? Shall we try?'

And with equal solemnity, the fourteen-year-old had nodded.

'My name's Patricia. Pat, to my friends.' She'd touched her lips with a forefinger, then touched the child's lips with that same finger. The passing of a kiss. The passing of a promise. 'No secrets, Sal?'

And the child had whispered, 'No secrets . . . Pat.'

Thus had started a relationship of rare beauty and real intimacy. There really *hadn't* been any secrets. In effect, they'd ganged up against Oldfield and knocked out of him whatever stuffiness his profession tended to impart.

'He's a smashing fella,' laughed Sal. 'A bit like dad, I suppose. Oh, I know his old man's – y'know . . .'

'A latter-day Bluebeard?' suggested Pat. 'Damn, where's that tartar sauce? Fish fingers are tasteless without tartar sauce.'

'Try the fridge.'

'Nobody in their right mind puts tartar sauce in a fridge.'

'You might. Anyway, he has this hang-up about his old man. Can't think why.'

'I can. Great heavens, you're right. I must have popped it in here when I stored this morning's milk.'

'How d'you mean, you can?'

'Child.' Pat closed the fridge, returned to the table, sat down and blathered her fish fingers with tartar sauce. 'He feels guilty by association. Anybody would.'

'I wouldn't. Why on earth do you bother with the fish fingers? Why not just blurp tartar sauce, and have done with it?'

'Because I need something with which to mop up the tartar sauce. And, anyway, I *hope* you would.'

'What?'

'Feel guilty by association. If you can feel happy because, you can feel sad because. Feeling guilty because, is the same thing.'

'Mmm. I suppose.'

It was Oldfield's 'Bridge Club Night' and, as always each fortnight, he snacked at a convenient cafe while the two women of his tiny family kitchen-scoffed in warm intimacy within reach of the Aga. Fish fingers – always fish fingers – because Sal liked fish fingers, Oldfield couldn't stand the damn things and Pat's digestive system would have made mincemeat of nuts and bolts. So, fish fingers, lashings of tartar sauce and a good old session of woman-talk.

'How do I know?' asked Sal solemnly. 'How do I know it's not a crush?'

'Bells ring,' grinned Pat.

'No, I'm serious. How *do* I know?'

'All right . . . serious.' Pat dabbed a tiny dribble of tartar sauce from one corner of her mouth with a paper napkin. 'Would you darn his old socks and think *he* was doing *you* a favour? Assuming *Love Story* was on one channel and *Match of the Day* was on the other, would you switch over without being asked and let him watch his infernal football? Without feeling martyred, I mean. If, like your dad, he was a jazz buff, would you let him shove *South Rampart Street* on at full blast and, even if you've a blinding headache, sit there with a dumb grin on your face and force one foot to keep time?'

'Boy, do you lead a grim life,' grinned Sal.

'You asked. It's not all chocolate and roses, that's what I'm getting at.'

'I must have a word with Dad,' teased Sal.

'What?'

'About *South Rampart Street*.'

'Don't you dare!' The grin matched that of her stepdaughter.

The banter continued throughout the meal; the give and take of waggery, but with an undercurrent of seriousness. Pat kept it from her tone and kept it from her eyes, but she was a little worried. This Rob Drever Sal was over the moon about. At an educated guess, *not* a crush; crushes didn't spawn these sort of questions; crushes equated with absolutes and certainties. In a back-to-front way, the very fact that she'd considered the possibility that it *was* a crush was near-proof that it *wasn't*. And if it was serious, well, he was still the son of his father.

Pat was no snap-judgement type. She could be wrong. She'd been wrong far too often in the past to have any illusions left as far as her own fallibility was concerned.

She said, 'Trot him around for a family inspection.'

'Dad might not like the idea . . .'

'Don't knock the old man. He isn't the stick-in-the-mud he

pretends to be.'

Sal hesitated, then said, 'Okay, when?'

'Sunday?' suggested Pat. 'For tea?'

'Oh, very antimacassar and lace curtains.'

'Fresh trout?' murmured Pat. 'Plus all the trimmings?'

'Ah!' Sal's eyes sparkled. 'The trout farm's open on a Sunday. I can pop up and buy in in the morning.' The sparkle left her eyes for a moment, and she said, 'Tell Dad, Pat. Warn him. Y'know ... what *not* to say.'

'Act and section, sweetheart.' Pat smiled. 'I'll draw up a list and make him learn it by heart.'

'Something wrong?'

Robert asked the question as he opened his mouth wide enough to take the first bite of the tomato and cheese sandwich. It was a rhetorical question; the slightly red-rimmed eyes and the hint of a quiver on the lower lip told their own story. On top of which as a brother and sister they were uncommonly close. The three-year gap didn't really exist. He was old for his age, she was young for her age. The two things made for a strange but perfect balance. As he chewed he watched her, and waited for an answer and, the answer, when it came, shattered him a little. It was so unlike the Anne he thought he knew so well.

'No, nothing wrong,' she snapped. 'I have a father who's a murderer, a mother who's tried to kill herself and a brother who can't arrive home on time. Why should there be anything *wrong*?'

'Hey, hold it.' His mouth was full of sandwich and he tended to spray. 'You me, too, remember. I mean something else wrong? Something I don't know about?'

She nodded and dropped onto a chair alongside the breakfast bar at which he sat. She remembered things; forced herself to remember things from the past. A solemn-faced younger brother, who, years ago, had earned himself the very whale of a licking from some foul-mouthed youth, five years his senior, because the foul-mouthed youth had made dirty remarks about the solemn-faced youngster's sister. That same kid brother who'd risked his neck climbing a half-dead elm in order to help down that same sister, who'd been too smart-arsed to know

79

which tree to climb and which tree not to climb. So many other things, too. Dozens of things. Scores of things.

She bit into the knuckle of a finger, in an attempt to prevent the blubbing. Not because Robert would have minded the blubbing, but because the elderly couple in the other room might hear and come to investigate. And for the moment *them* she could do without. All *they* did was try to be kind and twist the knife. All *they* had was love, but no understanding.

Robert cleared his mouth and said, 'Come on, sis. What's happened?'

'They – they want me to live with them,' she muttered, still keeping the knuckle in place between her teeth.

' "They"?'

'Gran and Gramp.'

'*Live* with them?'

She nodded.

'For *always*? Not just a holiday?' His voice was low but savage. Like his sister, the last thing he wanted was an interruption by one, or both, of their grandparents.

Again she nodded.

He lowered the sandwich onto the plate, then drank tea from the beaker. He seemed to be taking his time; letting the new development soak into his realisation before expressing an opinion.

He took a deep breath, expelled it, then whispered, 'Okay, they *mean* well, let's grant them that. Let's not go overboard. But they don't *understand*.'

She shook her head numbly. Still with the finger between her teeth.

'It wouldn't *help*,' he continued in a low voice. 'Christ, it would make things worse. Ten times worse. We wouldn't be a family any more.'

She blinked, lowered her hand, sniffed then said, 'They don't see things that way. I think . . .' She stopped.

'Yeah?'

'I – I think *they* think I'd be better – we'd both be better – away from mother.' She stared at him, wild-eyed for a moment, then breathed, 'Isn't that *awful*?'

'Liz . . . does she know?'

'No. They waited till she left for the hospital.'

'They're nice people,' he said. Neither of them wanted to be critical of their grandparents. 'They're on a different wavelength, that's all. I'll explain. They'll understand.'

'Will they?' She sounded doubtful.

'I'm going to be an architect.' He grinned a quick, but twisted, grin. 'If necessary, I can draw beautiful diagrams. I'll make them understand.'

He would, too. She hadn't any doubts. Once started, Robert could do anything. He way, his speed, but he'd *do* it.

In a decidedly less miserable voice, she said, 'Babs rang. She'll arrive later this evening.'

'That,' said Robert picking up the sandwich, 'is what we're short on . . . light relief.'

RAC and AA four-star recommended takes some living up to in the hotel world. It means fine food, expertly prepared and efficiently served; a good cellar, and a wine waiter who relies upon more than fractured English when asked for advice; a room service capable of turning Mary Poppins green with envy. All this and wall-to-wall luxury. Five-star is, of course, the tops, but only oil magnates, pop stars and the like can touch that fifth star and, outside the capital, a scouting party is required to *locate* that ultimate in hostelry. In the provinces four-star carries the torch and even then is not easy to find.

The Wounded Hart was four-star, and for a town as small as Beechwood Brook that too was a near-miracle. It was never full. On the other hand it was never empty. The brewery who owned this palace of delight figured (and to an extent rightly) that masochistically inclined holiday-makers, spending their spare time trudging around the nearby Tops, would welcome high-priced solace while they nursed their aching feet. Fiddling conventions used 'The Arrow Suite', wedding receptions favoured 'The Venison Lounge' and there was even an 'Antler Room' – all of 1700 square feet – wherein the blue-rinse ladies of the neighbourhood sat at tables, thrice a week, ignored the not-so-hot string quartet, hooked their little fingers as they drank tea and nibbled digestive biscuits and busied themselves keeping the local hot gossip circulating. Monday, Wednesday and Friday afternoons, the Antler Room saw more dirty washing exposed to view than any launderette.

When telephoned Ruth Linley had said certainly she'd meet them in the Greensward American Bar. Would eight o'clock be convenient? Fine. That would give her time to enjoy a meal then freshen herself up. Mind you, they mustn't expect too much. Carol Drever was the person she really wanted to see, but perhaps arrangements could be made when they'd had a chat.

'She sounded very reasonable,' said Liz as Bryant guided her through the carpeted lounge. He nodded a silent greeting to the snooty-looking female behind the reception desk, then glanced at the ornate signpost which pointed the way to various parts of the establishment.

'Secrecy and reasonableness,' he murmured. 'Not the sort of mixture I'm mad about.'

Liz didn't argue. It was nice having this droll, angular man as an escort; comforting, in that she was prepared to accept his assessment of whatever situation might develop. It made a pleasant change having somebody else around to make decisions.

He led her into the American bar; a room with a thick-piled, scarlet carpet around which were scattered glass-topped tubular-steel tables, and tubular-steel chairs upholstered in the same scarlet as the carpet. Around the walls were about a dozen deep armchairs; focal points about which tables and chairs might be moved. The bar was long and shiny, with an impressive array of booze reflected in a gilt-framed mirror which stretched the length of the bar-counter. A white-coated, bow-tied bar-keep was keeping his hands employed by polishing glasses already sparkling. A couple and a trio – man/woman, man/two women – were leaning forward over tables, talking in low voices and smiling. A woman sat alone in one of the armchairs in the far corner of the room. She saw them enter, glanced at the wall-clock, then raised mildly enquiring eyebrows.

She'd once been beautiful. That was Bryant's immediate impression. At a guess she was around the fifty mark, and even in a crowd she could still turn heads; beauty had plumped out a little into statuesque elegance, but the basic bone structure was there, and she'd looked after herself. No doubt the foundation garments had cost a bomb, and the pearl grey two-piece was no off-the-peg affair. Nevertheless, and accepting a whole wagon load of 'ifs' and 'buts', this one had been a *real* beauty in her day.

Thus the feelings of the man. Liz, on the other hand, felt an irrational surge of envy. Almost jealousy. Here was a woman who'd twisted men around her little finger. Still could at a guess. She had that indescribable air. That assurance which takes for granted that anything in pants is going to come running at the lift of an eyebrow.

As if to prove the point, the bar-keep arrived at the table.

'Miss Linley?' murmured Bryant.

'Yes. Doctor Bryant? Miss Stewart? Then having nodded their introductions, 'What will you have to drink?'

'Bitter lemon,' said Liz tightly.

'Nothing stronger?'

'Not at the moment.'

'And you, doctor?'

'Whisky, please. Fifty-fifty water.'

'And I'll have another brandy, please.'

'Yes, madam.' The bar-keep bobbed a quick gesture of subservience and disappeared.

They settled in their chairs around the low table and for a moment none of them spoke. Ruth Linley picked an opened packet of cigarettes from the table and offered them round. Bryant moved the heavy glass ash-tray to a point where all three could use it without effort and, by the time the cigarettes were lit, the drinks were on the table and the bar-keep had returned to his position behind the counter. The choice of position was perfect; as long as they kept their voices to an intimate, conversational level nobody else in the room could overhear what they were saying.

Ruth Linley said, 'It's good of you to come.'

'We're curious.' Liz's voice was still a little tight.

'And you, doctor?'

'Let's say ...' Bryant moved the cigarette. 'Moral support. And, of course, equal curiosity.'

'Because I asked him to come,' said Liz, and hoped Bryant would forgive and understand the white lie. It was necessary for her own ego; to demonstrate that she, too, could ask a mature man to do something without there necessarily being a refusal.

'My intention was to speak to your sister.'

'That's out of the question.'

'Eventually,' insisted Linley gently.

Bryant said, 'Not for some time. She's – er . . .'

'She tried to commit suicide,' said Liz bluntly.

Surprisingly Linley frowned before murmuring, 'That's understandable.'

'It was damned silly.'

'Ah, but you, as a doctor, must dismiss everything as 'silly' unless it reacts to salve, injection or medicine.'

And that (thought Liz) puts you in your place, Doctor Bryant. And at this point some of the stiffness left her.

She said, 'Miss Linley, my sister and I are close. Very close. I've lived with her – with her and William – since shortly after they were married. We've no secrets. None at all. And . . .' She hesitated, then ended, 'I'm here to protect her.'

'From me?' Ruth Linley looked slightly amused.

'You must have a motive,' said Bryant gruffly. 'You're the mother of one of the murdered girls . . . or so you claim.'

'Oh, indeed I am.' She nodded solemnly. 'The mother of the third girl to be murdered then mutilated.'

'Therefore, you must have a motive.'

'Not a motive . . . a *reason*.'

'Same thing.'

'Not at all, doctor.' For some reason, she seemed to be deliberately terse with Bryant. With something of a shock, Liz realised the possibility that the sharp manner was this woman's way of conveying to *her* the fact that she wasn't interested in impressing the angular medic. Was, in fact, throwing out 'Keep Off' signals in his direction. Linley continued, 'Reason and motive. The same difference as between indigestion and ulcers.'

Bryant breathed heavily, then took a long swig from his drink.

'I don't like answering to the name Miss Linley.' This with an engaging smile to Liz. 'My friends call me Ruth. My enemies use any name they care to think up, I couldn't care less.'

'Your enemies,' said Liz quietly.

'You're not one of them.' Again the engaging smile. 'Neither is your sister.'

'All right . . . Ruth.'

84

'And may I call you Liz?'

'I – er – I suppose so.'

'Everybody else does.'

'All right . . . *Liz*.'

'How,' began Bryant, 'do *you* know everybody . . .'

'Tell me about William.' The words cut across what Bryant was going to say. 'You've lived with your sister since shortly after she was married. Which means you've lived under the same roof as William. You must have reached certain conclusions. Certain opinions. I'd be very interested.'

'Obviously, I . . .' Liz stopped, sipped at her drink, then began again. 'Obviously, I didn't know him as well as I *thought* I knew him. The – er – the murders. Your daughter. That was a shock. A tremendous shock.'

'Forget the murders.' Ruth smiled. '*Try* to forget the murders. Your opinion of him *before* he was arrested?'

'He's always been kind to me,' said Liz awkwardly. Then hurriedly, 'But don't misconstrue that. As a brother-in-law. Nothing more. He's given me a home. Given me comfort – a comfortable living – even a weekly allowance. That sort of thing.'

'And in return?'

'Well, I – y'know ... I suppose I've been unofficial housekeeper. Unofficial nursemaid when the children were younger. I've taken as much burden as possible from Carol's shoulders.'

'A sight too much,' grunted Bryant, as if he was privy to the workings of the Drever family.

'And the man, William? Domineering? Masterful? Sycophantic? Weak? Boastful? The overall impression over the years?'

'He can't defend himself.' Liz stared at the glass top of the table. In what was little more than an unhappy mutter she said, 'I was wrong. A lot of people were wrong. But I won't criticise him for – y'know – other things. Not when he isn't here to defend himself.'

'Loyalty,' murmured Ruth.

'What's wrong with that?'

'Nothing, Doctor Bryant. Nothing at all. But logic insists that, if Liz here, won't criticise him because he isn't here to answer the criticism, there must *be* criticism.'

'He has a wife.' Bryant seemed to move into a position in which he formed a barrier between the probing questions of Ruth, and the reluctance of Liz to answer those questions. 'She made an abortive attempt at suicide. At least she went through the motions. Wrist-slashing ... not the quickest, not the easiest way. But a very messy way. It always *looks* far worse than it is.'

'You're trying to express an opinion, doctor.'

'I am.' Bryant nodded, then drew on his cigarette. 'Attempted suicide with three people in the house. At night, but a night following a very emotional day. It was no gamble. It was a dead cert that *one* of those people would still be awake.'

'Therefore *not* an attempt at suicide?'

'She wanted sympathy,' growled Bryant.

'She *had* sympathy,' muttered Liz. 'God knows, she had all the sympathy in the world.'

'Doctor?' Ruth raised one eyebrow.

'All right.' Bryant waved the cigarette. 'She *had* sympathy. Like when a person dies ... for a few days everybody ignores the bad things. But after a while – when the numbness wears off – they tend to remember. The true perspective returns. Carol Drever had sympathy galore. More sympathy than she deserved, that at a guess. The wrist-slashing episode. She could have been stock-piling sympathy. Knowing she might need it when ...' He moved his shoulders.

'When the numbness wears off?' suggested Ruth and a wry smile touched her lips.

Like animals on a vivisection table, thought Liz angrily. They can't answer back. They can't struggle. They don't even know what's happening. Carol and William being slashed and hacked, probed and examined by two strangers. It was *obscene*.

'You two,' she choked. 'Stop it! They've gone through hell. Both of them. Yes, William too. And – and you sit here and calmly ...'

'*My daughter was murdered, then mutilated.*'

The icy statement of fact, although soft-spoken, was like a slap in the face. It brought reality down to earth with a bump. The basic reason for them being there. The reason for Drever being in prison and his wife being in a hospital ward. Compared with these things talk – mere talk, irregardless of what that talk was about – was as nothing. An academic frippery. A pointless discussion about hunger in the presence of a starving man.

Liz tried to speak, but her mouth was too dry. She tipped what was left of the bitter lemon down her throat with a quick, slightly hysterical movement. Bryant cleared his throat, squashed out his cigarette, then stood up.

He said, 'I'll – er – I'll get some more drinks.' To Ruth Linley. 'Same again?'

'Please.' And the calm politeness was back in place again.

'Liz?'

'Bloody Mary.' And the venom made it sound like a mild curse.

Bryant pushed his chair back, picked up the empty glasses and walked to the counter.

Very gently Ruth Linley said, 'Have patience, Liz. There's a reason.'

'I'm sorry.' The pale face, the swimming eyes, combined with the expression to show the depths of her wretchedness. 'I shouldn't have . . .' Then, in little more than a whisper. 'We seem to forget the *other* family. Our own misery. Our own shame. I suppose it always happens.'

Robert told them. He didn't mince words; he knew of no way to ease what he had to say. He didn't set out to hurt, but he knew he was hurting. But on the other hand he didn't have to draw his 'beautiful diagrams'.

Mary Drever took it the worst. Not, perhaps, because of the plan to give a home to Anne was being rejected, but rather because Robert was voicing the rejection. Robert was very special to her; a re-run of William, but this time without the mistakes they'd made in the past.

'You shouldn't say such things,' she sniffed.

'Gran.' The eighteen-year-old placed an arm around the elderly woman he'd had to hurt. 'You mean well. You're nice people and we love you. But we're a family, and we can't split up.'

'That bloody Liz!' growled Bill Drever . . . and that was the one thing he *shouldn't* have said.

That grunted escape of indignation from Bill Drever started the row. That he didn't really mean it; that, in his eyes, Liz was

87

a far better woman that her sister; that the angry exclamation was merely the outward manifestation of a man well on in years who'd once held sway over his own little empire. All this meant nothing. The three words were the detonator which triggered off the explosive agrument.

What did you mean? They knew perfectly well what it meant; that Liz had grown to have more say in the running of the house than their own mother. What was wrong with Liz? What had Liz ever done to deserve that sort of remark? Liz wasn't their mother, that was what was wrong and, if their mother had been anything like a good mother, she wouldn't have allowed things to get to this pass. Mother was in hospital – had they forgotten that? – and without Liz heaven only knew how they'd have coped. They'd have coped easily enough, if only they'd been brought up properly; if only their mother had been interested enough in making a home and bringing up a family.

'And that from *you*?' Anne's eyes blazed, and she almost screamed the accusation. 'You two "brought up" a murderder, and now you want *me* to come and live with you.'

Robert groaned, 'Oh my God, sis!' You shouldn't have *said* that,' but it was too late, it had been said and, anyway, Anne didn't hear, she was rushing from the room and upstairs, to throw herself across the bed and there sob her anger and heartbreak into submission.

The grandson and the grandparents stared at each other in thick silence. It had all been said. Too much had been said. However hard they tried, it would never be forgotten.

Robert felt cheap. Soiled. He remembered all those other rows. The rows carried on in make-believe secrecy behind closed doors. The shouting and screaming. The insults and the unforgivable accusations.

'Liz, why do they *do* this?'

'They don't *mean* it, Robert. It's part of being married.'

'But it's wrong. People shouldn't . . .'

'Come on downstairs, Robert. It'll be over soon.'

Poor Liz. Dear Liz. Always ready with the excuses. But it had never been over 'soon'. Days, sometimes weeks, of cold, bitten-off conversations; a poor effort at normal behaviour for the benefit of Anne and himself. Snide remarks and tightened lips.

Silly little phrases which, given the right emphasis, had the wounding power of a sniper's bullets. 'But of course.' 'It's an opinion.' 'I wouldn't dream of contradicting an expert.' Dozens of them, each snapped off and each hitting the target.

One thing for sure, when *he* married . . .

'Liz, can't you *make* them be friends?'

'I only live here, pet. Give it time. It'll pass.'

Meanwhile, Gran was blinking. Quickly; like a windscreen wiper switched to double speed. Seeming to refuse the tears an exit, but crying like crazy inside. Gramp was red in the face. Lips closed but working, like a writhing worm. Eyes quietening a little from the blazing fury of a moment ago. He raised a hand, and the back of the hand across his mouth. A gesture. 'Body language'. An erasure of the words hurled without a thought at his grandchildren.

Robert cleared his throat and croaked, 'Er – whisky, Gramp?'

'Eh?'

'Whisky?' He moved his hands in helpless, fluttering gestures. 'We – we don't *mean* to hurt each other. None of us. Have a – have a whisky . . . please.'

'Aye.' Bill Drever tried to smile; a man-to-man, worldly smile, which didn't quite reach his eyes. 'Aye, why not?'

'Gran?'

'Nothing for me.' The single shake of the head refused any attempt at reconciliation.

'Please.'

'No.'

'Bring her a brandy, lad,' grunted Bill Drever. 'A nice, stiff brandy. It's what she needs.'

Four more people – two couples – had entered the Greensward American Bar, but the cunning of the positioned tables still ensured enough privacy for the talk to continue. Gentle talk. Very civilised talk. Yet terrifying, because of its subject-matter and because it *was* gentle and civilised.

Quite calmly Ruth Linley said, 'They were diseased. It came out in court. They were all three diseased.'

'It – er – it said so in the newspapers,' said Liz awkwardly.

'They *were*.' She sounded positive. Then, 'The first two, pox.

89

My daughter, clap.'

Liz felt shocked. The words – the street-corner slang – sounded doubly foul when spoken by this educated, well-dressed woman. The words shocked, because the enunciation was perfect.

Ruth Linley turned to Bryant and said, 'You've examined Carol Drever?'

'Not for *that*.' Bryant scowled. He, too, was shocked at the sudden turn in the conversation. 'Anything like that, and she'd have consulted her own G.P.'

'Liz?' Ruth moved her head.

Liz looked puzzled.

'Has she visited her doctor, recently?'

'I . . . wouldn't know. That sort of thing . . .' Liz felt the colour rising from her neck. 'People don't talk about . . .' She closed her mouth.

'You claim to have been close,' Ruth reminded her.

'We were. But that sort of thing . . .'

'I'll find out,' said Bryant quietly. 'A blood test. She needn't know why.'

'She'll be clean,' pronounced Ruth with a half-smile. 'William was. They don't pussyfoot around those questions in prison.'

Bryant said, 'How the hell do *you* know?'

'So many things.' The half-smile again, then, 'Contacts, doctor.' She drew deeply on her cigarette, then mused, 'A point that might have been made in his defence.'

'It doesn't *prove* anything,' said Bryant.

'Nevertheless a hint. A straw in the wind.' Again an inhalation of cigarette smoke, followed by a taste of her drink then, still musingly, 'The Copycat Ripper'. Such an obscene tag. I'll wager it rolls off Snout's typewriter without him even touching the keys.'

'Snout?'

'The fat man, Liz. The obese pig standing guard at your gate.'

'Oh, him.'

'Him.' She nodded, finished her drink in one last gulp, then changed her mood. Businesslike. Challenging. 'William . . . you accepted the verdict?'

'Of course.'

'You? Carol? Anne and Robert? Even his parents?'

'Of course,' repeated Liz.

'He pleaded "Not Guilty". You obviously didn't believe him.'

'They convicted.' Liz felt the slight tremor in her voice. The slight touch of hope she daren't acknowledge. 'The jury convicted.'

'And you believe twelve strangers rather than the man you claim to know so well?'

'You're leading up to something,' said Bryant in a mildly accusing tone.

'Indeed.' She nodded. 'That's why we're here. A proposition, doctor. A proposition based upon the trial. Based upon the evidence. If he killed one, he killed all three?'

'Of course.' He nodded solemnly.

'If he *didn't* kill one, he *didn't* kill any?'

'I follow the argument,' said Bryant carefully.

'But you don't agree?'

'Yes.' Bryant hesitated, then seemed to take the plunge. 'Let's say I agree. It's hardly logical to accept one proposition and not accept the other.'

Very calmly Ruth Linley said, 'He didn't kill my daughter.'

'How ...' Liz found herself breathing hard. As if she'd just completed a toiling race. 'How do you know he didn't ...'

'I'm not prepared to believe he committed incest, then murdered, then mutilated his own child. He knew. He knew who she was. He loved her.' She paused then, in a low, hard voice – a voice admitting no possibility of doubt – she said, 'William Drever didn't kill her.'

My own view of the Ten Command-
ments is very like that of an Anglican
Bishop who once said that they are
like an examination paper – eight
only to be attempted.

*Muggeridge Through The
Microphone*
                    Malcolm Muggeridge

Bryant stared ahead through the rain-washed windscreen of the Peugeot, and in some curious way his heart-beat seemed to keep perfect time with the steady sweep of the wipers. Medically, of course, it was ridiculous; other than at a pulse-point nobody could monitor the beat of their own heart. But come to that, everything of this evening was ridiculous. The woman sitting beside him wasn't his patient. Nor was her sister. The same with her brother-in-law. The same with the woman Ruth Linley. None of them his patients, yet he'd wager he knew more about them all than their own medics. Not their ailments, not their past medical histories, but *them* ... as people.

It was, of course, all wrong. Ethically, he hadn't a leg to stand on. He was trespassing on the preserves of fellow-doctors, and the chances were they wouldn't be amused. Assuming they ever found out, of course. In short, he was a silly old buffer, shoving his nose into things not of his concern. But, so what? He was old enough to mind other people's business if the whim so took him.

Liz, for example, fascinated him. A sweet mix of self-assurance and vulnerability. Honest with everybody except herself. The dumb female who'd slashed her wrist didn't deserve a sister like Liz. Didn't deserve somebody willing and able to iron out the bumps of everyday life. All *that* one deserved was a swift spanking; a spoiled child ready for the back of a hairbrush.

And the Linley woman. Was it possible to be *too* honest? Objectivity was a fine thing, but couldn't it be carried *too* far? And if she'd known William Drever was innocent, why had she kept quiet? Why had she let him stand trial, much less be convicted? Wheels within wheels within wheels, old son. And even wheels within *those* wheels. God made women ... and only He could understand 'em.

As for Drever. A man facing a murder charge, and he doesn't tell everything? He doesn't come up with the one defence likely to work? For some obscure 'Beau Geste' reason, maybe? Fine. It made good reading. But in real life? And, if in real life, with a man like William Drever? Damn it, what was he getting his brain into a spin about? He didn't know the man. Hadn't met him. Hadn't even *seen* him, much less spoken to him. But – again, dammit – he *did* know him. Through the eyes, words and actions of three women, he *did* know him. A stupid, self-opinionated tripehound

95

. . . that for sure. A man who couldn't keep his own wife in order. A man willing to let his wife's sister take on the dirty work for a pittance and a roof to sleep under. A man who put other women in the family way, then kept quiet about it and allowed his natural daughter to grow up into a whore. My God! Did he know him? Or, if not him, personally, his kind?

The reds and whites and flashing ambers of other vehicles were reflected and elongated in the wet road surface. The lighted windows, too. And the traffic lights. A black and shiny world, spangled with moving and changing fairy-lights. A watery grotto through which the warm interior of the car swam, surrounded by cold torches of changing hue. And inside the car the colours were reflected and softened.

The colours touched the moisture of the tears running silently down her cheeks, and when he saw them it was with a sense of real shock.

'Now then, now then.' He tried to divide his attention between driving the car and comforting the woman alongside him. 'It's all right, lassie. She doesn't mean anybody any harm. I'm convinced of that.'

'She's so right.' She sat upright. Primly, her hands resting on her lap, making no effort to wipe away the tears. 'She's so very right.'

'I'm sorry, I . . . Damn and blast it, woman! Can you not give *some* sort of a bloody signal?' This to an unknown woman driver who turned her car right and directly into the path of the Peugeot. Then, having braked and swerved slightly, he said, 'Sorry. We'll pull in, then we can talk.'

'We didn't believe him,' she said softly. 'Instead, we believed twelve strangers who didn't even *know* him.'

'Lassie, you can't seriously blame yourself for . . .'

'Please don't keep calling me "lassie".' The voice was still soft but it had an edge. 'I'm not a "lassie", I'm a middle-aged woman.'

'Miss Stewart.'

'Liz. Everybody else. Why not you?'

'All right . . . Liz.'

There was a public house on the left and alongside it a car park with a shaded and unoccupied corner. Bryant steered the

Peugeot into the corner, parked and turned off the lights.

He half-turned in his seat, and said, 'All right, Liz. You've carried a load for a long time. A lot of it not your own. You've heard something from a woman – a woman you don't know from Adam – and one of the things she's said has made you think. Hurt you. D'you think it wasn't *meant* to hurt you?'

'*Meant* to hurt me?'

Bryant realised it was only a straw. Perhaps not even that. A devil's advocacy; a deliberate slanting of the facts in order to give false comfort and make-believe solace. But, straw or not, she clutched at it, and he argued from what he knew was a very shaky premise.

'Think about her,' her urged. 'Quite calmly, quite cold-bloodedly she takes for granted the fact that her daughter's on the game. A prostitute. More than that even. A prostitute diseased with gonorrhoea. What sort of a woman? What sort of a mother? I don't give a hoot who the girl's father was. William ... anybody. That the mother – *any* mother – could calmly sit there and make such an admission ... Liz, every word she said was meant to hurt.'

'I ...' She sniffed. 'I don't think so. I think she's ... different. That's all. Different from the rest of us.'

'Different, in that she's complete contempt for the British Legal System?'

'We *should* have believed,' she whimpered.

'Why?' He was fighting. Fighting hard. But very gradually he was winning. It might be only a temporary victory, but however slight, however temporary it was very necessary. 'Why?' he repeated. 'Because a woman like that *says* so? Because by implication – by *her* implication – the police, the courts, the witnesses, everybody is corrupt and rotten. Liz! Liz! Of course he denied the charge. They *all* do. Guilty or innocent. But when everything – *everything* – pointed to his guilt. Don't blame yourself for accepting what the whole world accepted. He was *found* guilty. He had lawyers. He was defended. On the face of it, it was an honest verdict. It you must blame somebody, blame that infernal woman. She could have saved him. Merely by coming forward she could have cast enough doubt on the police case. But she didn't ... and, dammit, now she's talked *you* into feeling disloyal.'

He was (and he knew it) a cunning old devil. Given a strong enough reason, he could argue any proposition in the world; that black was merely a dark shade of white; that up was merely less deep than down. It was a knack, and he'd used it a thousand times in the past when dealing with certain types of patient.

He twisted the words Ruth Linley had used. Used the limited capacity of Liz's remembrance to turn the phrases inside out and, having done so, built up a picture of an embittered woman, hiding her bitterness beneath a smooth and expensive exterior. Strong-willed and sly. An artist at saying one thing, but meaning another.

And, gradually, he won through. The tears stopped. She wiped her eyes and blew her nose. He lighted two cigarettes, then passed one to her, and they smoked in shadowed silence in the corner of the car park. The swing of headlights from an arriving or departing car occasionally illuminated the interior of the Peugeot, but their privacy remained intact.

She squashed out her cigarette and said, 'What time is it?' and her voice was at its usual steady norm.

He glanced at the luminous dial of his watch and said, 'Half nine ... almost.'

'We'd better get back.'

'Why?' He seemed unwilling to break the intimacy he'd worked so hard to create.

'Babs. William's sister. She's coming up from London.'

'Good.' He, too, squashed out his cigarette. 'She can take some of the weight from your shoulders.'

'That, I doubt,' she smiled. 'That I very much doubt. You don't know Babs.'

Babs Drever. Strictly speaking, Barbara Drever, but even on the credits it was always 'Babs Drever'. She figured herself to be the original swinging chick, and this despite the forty-odd years she had tucked away behind the gilt-linked chain which circled her waist. The one and only honey-pot, from her expensive 'urchin-style' hair-do to the blood-coloured lacquer which peeped from open-toed sandals. God's gift to half the human race ... the male half, of course.

Mary Drever kept her mouth tightly closed, other than when she took ever so dainty sips at the brandy Robert had handed her. This daughter of hers was well beyond her comprehension. Asked, she would have called her a 'fast little cat' without a second's hesitation because with daughters – as opposed to daughters-in-law – one need not moderate either language or opinion. Bill Drever – who was on his second whisky and his second pipe of tobacco – quite deliberately turned on his 'do it for thi' sen' voice; the thick dialect of rural Yorkshire, knowing that it annoyed this wayward, London-oriented child of his loins.

'*Fabulous*!' Babs gushed more often than she spoke. Gushed in exclamation marks to the accompaniment of fluttering fingers or waving arms. She was talking primarily to Robert and was describing her journey north. 'The way Clint can handle that Merc. You wouldn't believe!'

'Clint?' rumbled Bill Drever.

'Like Clint Eastwood, Gramp,' grinned Robert.

'Who the 'ell's he, when he's at home?'

'Father! You're positively cave-age.'

'He's a film star,' explained Robert. 'A very good film star.'

'Oh, aye? Like James Mason?'

'Well, no, not a bit like James Mason.'

'Wi' a name like that ...' And the grunted half-finished sentence dismissed all non-Yorkshire-born actors as jumped up whippersnappers who didn't know the footlights from the foyer.

'Where's Carol?' asked Babs.

She asked the question of Robert, and Robert averted his eyes and looked awkward.

'She tried to do hersen' in,' said Bill.

'She *what*!' She almost shrieked the last word.

'She had a go at her wrist with a razor blade,' muttered Robert. 'Liz found her in time. That's were Liz is now. At the hospital. Checking that things are okay.'

'What a *ghastly* thing to do.'

'Sit thi' sen' down,' growled Bill. 'Prancing about like a bloody circus pony. Tha's making t' place look untidy.'

'Why the hell aren't *you* there?' She spun on her father and for the moment all the fluffy-mindedness was pushed aside. It was a Babs new to them. A Babs who, despite sleeping around a lot,

99

wasn't quite the madcap she pretended to be. Within the cut-throat world of television she'd made a name. The hard way, and now it showed. She turned to Mary Drever and snapped, 'You, too. Why the hell aren't *you* there?'

Mary Drever's nostrils quivered, but she didn't answer.

Babs stormed, 'A mad brother, who shoves knives into cheap slags. Somebody they'll find a place for in The Chamber of Horrors. And now, you two ...'

'*Ah, but he didn't.*' When Babs claimed centre-stage earthquakes went unnoticed. Therefore Liz was already in the room, unbelting her mac and teasing her slightly dampened hair. She was the only person moving. The others formed a gape-mouthed tableau. Waiting. Holding their breath. Wondering what was coming next. Liz said, 'I have it on very good authority. *He didn't.*'

'What authority?' croaked Bill Drever.

'The mother of the third victim,' said Liz calmly. 'She's quite categorical. William pleaded "Not Guilty" because he *wasn't* guilty.'

The matron locked in to check that the Dalmane capsule was doing its trick. The lips weren't quite as bloodless and the half-moon bruises under the eyes had almost gone. The rubber soles of her shoes made a squeaking noise on the lino, and the eyelids fluttered.

'Go back to sleep.' The matron leaned down and straightened the bedclothes. It was an automatic movement, born of a lifetime of nursing.

'I wasn't asleep.'

'Almost.'

'No, just thinking.'

'Go to sleep, dear.'

Just thinking. Remembering. Re-living. '... to be your lawfully wedded wife ... till death ...' Ah, yes, but *whose* death? His death? My death? The death of three unknown women? 'I'd like to talk.'

'I have my rounds to do.'

'Please.'

'You must go to sleep, dear.'

'Can I please have a glass of water?'

What Robert used to say. The excuse of every child in the world. 'Mummy, can I have a drink of water?' He'll make a fine architect. But no, he *won't*. Not any more. No money. No future. No anything . . . for *anybody*.

'You should go to sleep.'

'Sit and talk. Please. Five minutes. No more than five minutes.'

'Not a second longer.' The matron made a sigh, pulled a chair nearer, then glanced at her watch before she sat down. 'Not one second longer than five minutes.'

'Do people often . . .' Carol raised her bandaged wrist a few inches from the counterpane.

'One is too many,' fenced the matron.

'Yes but . . . you know what I mean.'

'You're not the first. You won't be the last.'

'I wonder why.' Her eyes went slightly out of focus, and she seemed to be searching for the answer, spelled out in the middle distance.

'It's very wrong. People should want to live.'

Live? Live how? Live where? The great medical con trick. Birth – life – death . . . three separate entities. Like a sandwich. The meaty bit was in the middle. The enjoyable bit. But what if the meat was off? 'Unfit for human consumption'? What if the slices of bread – one of the slices – tasted far better than the filling?

In the silent distance of the hospital a telephone bell started to ring. The patter of hurrying footsteps. A door opening, then the bell stopped ringing.

The matron was saying, '. . . a fine sister. Two fine children. You've everything to live for.'

Liz. Always back to Liz. Always the comparison. Liz had sense; good sense; too much sense to end up in a hospital bed with everybody contemptuous, but play-acting sympathy. Liz was a mirror-image of what every good wife *should* be. But if you lived with that mirror? If you were never allowed to take your eyes from that mirror?

'Liz never married,' she murmured.

'It isn't everything. I've never married . . . nor intend to.'

'It's over-rated.'

'I think you should go to sleep.'

'It changes you. Changes you completely.'

'I think I'd better . . .'

'No! You said five minutes.'

The matron relaxed back onto the chair and sighed.

William . . . the gawky, awkward William. The gawky, awkward slayer. But not at first. At first the gawky, awkward husband. Needing to be advised. Needing to be dominated. 'William, you're a grown man. Don't act like a child.' But *not* a child. *Never* a child. A gawky, awkward husband and, hiding inside − crouching in some secret corner − a gawky, awkward mass-murderer.

'I wouldn't have minded,' she breathed.

'What?'

'If it had been men.'

'Look, dear, you really must go to . . .'

'If they hadn't been whores.'

'Sleep,' said the matron firmly. She stood up, re-positioned the chair and brushed her palm across the already creaseless counterpane. 'Sleep's what you need. What your body needs. What your brain needs. Think about nice things. About your sister and about your children. And go to sleep.'

Liz . . . everything she could never be. Anne − a younger edition of her mother perhaps − and God help her if all this was part of her future. Robert − a younger edition of his father perhaps − and God help *everybody* if . . .'

'I wish . . .' she began.

But the matron was no longer there. Only an empty side-ward, with the glow of a night-light bulb illuminating the sparse furnishings. And a woman − a wretched, unhappy woman, called Carol Drever − alone with 'nice' thoughts.

'Right,' said Bill Drever, 'we'd better sort out who *did* kill 'em.'

He made it sound easy. As obvious as a single tarmac path through a forest. To Bill Drever it *was* easy. All life was easy, unless you complicated things. Like building. Good bricks, good mortar, a plumb-line and a spirit level. You shoved one brick on top of, or alongside, another. Eventually, you had a house. Like life; straight up, straight down, keep things nice and even, one day on top of, or alongside, another. Eventually, all your worries were things of the past. Unless, of course, you had an idiot for a son and a lunatic for a daughter. Things like that buggered things up. But it wasn't *your* fault. Left to yourself, things would have been easy.

It was a council of war. They believed Liz and what Liz had told them about the conversation with Ruth Linley. Partly because they wanted to believe, but mainly because Liz was obviously so sure.

A red-eyed Anne, brought down from her bedroom, had raised token objection.

'Why didn't Daddy call her as a witness?'

It was a question not seriously answered nor, indeed, seriously answerable without further facts, but Babs had provided an answer of a sort.

'Lawyers! They play court-house games. They can screw a good case rotten with their fancy tactics.'

Such was their anxiety to counter their previous lack of faith in William Drever's plea that they accepted the opinion as a good enough reason.

Mary Drever had, of course, been shocked.

'His daughter? His own daughter? That I'll never believe. I brought my lad up better than *that*.'

'To be a murderer?' mocked Babs.

'Nay. Liz has just said . . .'

'You can't have the cake *and* the cherry, Ma. She's either his bastard or he's knifed three strangers.'

And that had disposed of *that* objection.

And now Bill Drever said, 'Right, we'd better sort out who *did* kill 'em.'

'We tell the police,' said Robert. 'Go to Lessford tomorrow, and tell the police they've made a mistake.'

'Not that easy, Robert my child.' Babs smoked slim cheroots. She held one between manicured fingers and, as she waved her hand, the blue-grey smoke cut temporary streamers in the air. 'First of all, the cops didn't convict him. The court, right? The cops can't ring up the judge and say, "Sorry, buster, we did it all wrong". For the moment brother William is in the schnook and there . . .'

'For God's sake,' grumbled Bill Drever, 'talk English.'

'Okay,' snapped Babs. 'He's in the can. To get him out of the can, we have to convince a lot of people that he shouldn't be *in* the can. Not the cops. They're *never* going to be convinced . . .'

'We can *start* with the police,' said Liz.

'Wasted time, honey.' Again the cheroot manufactured smoke ribbons. 'Nobody is going to listen. Cops are human. They're right *because* they're right. The best reason in the world for never being wrong.'

'This Linley woman,' suggested Anne.

'Are they going to believe her? Just like that?'

Bill Drever said, 'There should be a birth certificate.'

'Bill!' protested his wife.

'Dammit, woman, whichever side of the blanket, there's a birth certificate.'

Such talk. So many ideas, some fanciful, some practical, some plucked straight from the pages of cheap fiction.

'Father, the Sam Spades of this world are grimy little back-street yobs who serve writs and peep through bedroom keyholes. Not murder for Christ's sake!'

And Babs, because of her worldy wisdom, gradually became the accepted oracle. Equally Liz became her second-in-command. Liz had brought hope. Certain tatty strings were attached to that hope to be sure – an illegitimate child was something the gutter-press would headline – but better that than 'The Copycat Ripper'.

'He's still a bloody disgrace.'

'Father, we don't *all* suffer from migraine brought on by tight haloes.'

At ten-thirty the elder Drevers stood up and announced their intention of leaving.

'We've a drive in front of us.'

'You can stay the night,' offered Liz.

'Nay . . . I like my own bed. Get your coat on, Mother.' Then to Babs, 'Happen it's as well you *are* here.'

'It's as well somebody's here.' Then with slightly narrowed eyes and a cool edge to her voice, 'When you reach your "own bed" don't go straight to sleep. Think about William. And Carol.

Force yourself. Ask yourself "why" a few dozen times.'

Which was a question posed by David Oldfield. A question rooted in anxiety that his daughter wasn't going to be hurt. Added to which, he'd suffered some particularly bad hands that evening at his Bridge Club. His, then, was a questioning mood; a mood not readily reconciled with harsh facts of life.

Why had it to be this Robert Drever youth?

Pat Oldfield explained, with some patience, that such a question admitted of no straightforward answer. Love – and especially young love – was a little like measles. No respecter of persons. It arrived and that's all there was to it. Fine, but why did Pat think this Sal/Robert thing was more serious than the usual teenage boy/girl friendship? Because Sal said so, and because she (Pat) credited Sal with knowing exactly how many beans made five. Because she (Pat) had never seen Sal so absolutely sure about anything in her life before. Nevertheless, why this Robert Drever youth? At Sal's age notoriety – even reflected notoriety – held certain attractions, didn't it? With some girls, but not with Sal. How could they be sure? She (Pat) *was* sure. She (Pat) was obviously tuned in to Sal's wavelength. Sal *knew* and she (Pat) *knew* Sal knew.

'Which,' said David Oldfield, 'is pure feminine logic. Utterly illogical.'

'Darling, she has it bad,' pleaded Pat. 'Not because of what he is. Because of *who* he is. For the moment he's the man in her life.'

'Man?'

'She's only seventeen. At seventeen, an eighteen-year-old is a man.'

' "For the moment"?'

'Forever starts with that time-span. It did with me. Why shouldn't it work the same with Sal?'

In the Drever household midnight passed and a quiltwork of decisions were arrived at. That, despite her objections, Babs would call at Lessfield Police Headquarters, and there float the proposition that the wrong man had been arrested and convicted.

'They won't believe you . . .'

'Too damn right they won't.'

'. . . but if you play your cards right, you might collect names. Witnesses. With luck people not called at the trial who might have something to add to what we already know.'

That Robert should attend Bordfield Polytech as usual.

'There must be *something* I can do to help.'

'Child, you're out-voted.'

'I'm not a child. Liz, tell her . . .'

'Robert.' The gentle smile neither Robert nor Anne could argue against. 'You're the only one left. The potential bread-winner. We'll try. But . . .' The slight movement of the shoulders. 'It's not going to be easy. It's not going to be soon. Maybe months. Maybe years. Maybe *never*. We need an eventual long-stop. You're *it*.'

Those two words, 'maybe never', measured the sheer magnitude of their task. To overturn the law. To reverse a Crown Court decision, not on some legal quibble, but on basic fact. The wrong man had been arrested, the wrong man had been accused, the wrong man had been convicted, the wrong man was serving a prison sentence.

It was agreed that wall slogans and petitions were out. Handbills were out. Interviews, in the press or on television, were out. 'Sure, I could fix it. But they're counter-productive. Who the hell *cares*?. Our policemen are wonderful. Nobody arguing from a glass screen ever screwed up that holy belief.' It was, therefore, a family fight. With energy, with guile but most of all with patience.

Babs drew deeply on her cheroot, then said, 'It's a Home Secretary job.'

Anne's eyes widened and she gasped, 'God, I hadn't realised . . .'

'You'd *better* realise, honey. Laughing Boy William stays put until we convince the Home Secretary no less that this whole screw-up is just that . . . a screw-up. And Home Secretaries don't want to know. They're deaf, dumb and blind until they have to do a breast stroke to keep on top of the effluent. Then they make noises. Self-preservation noises.'

It was agreed, therefore, that Robert should continue his studies and Anne should return to her place behind the counter of a travel agency. And having agreed upon this (but little else) the two youngsters took their leave and went to bed. Liz and Babs relaxed a little; the pressure was off; the mock-up of we'll-do-it-or-bust, put on for the benefit of William's parents and William's children, was by mutual understanding pushed aside. Liz padded off in stocking feet to percolate fresh coffee. 'And make it strong and hot, honey. With room for a nice splash of brandy.' Alone and very unladylike Babs planted her feet on the hearthrug, lowered the seat of her snazzy trousers to the top of her thighs and, with all the vulgarity with which she had carved a niche for herself on the fringe of the showbiz world, allowed the cheeks of her backside to turn a rosy pink from the heat of the electric fire. She was still there when Liz returned with the coffee, and Liz grinned friendly approval.

'All girls together,' murmured Babs and hoisted the trousers back into position again. As Liz splashed brandy into the beakers of coffee, Babs flopped into one of the armchairs and said, 'And now, the kissing stops and the screwing starts. You want an opinion?'

'It's not going to be easy.' Liz carried the breakers to the hearth and handed one to Babs.

'We haven't a hope in hell.' Babs sipped at the coffee, then placed the beaker on the carpet alongside the armchair. She placed a cheroot between her lips, and it wobbled as she added, 'Between us two, of course.'

'It'll take time. It'll take patience.'

'It'll take a bloody miracle.'

Babs lighted the cheroot. Liz took a cigarette from the box on the mantlepiece, lighted it, blew out smoke, lowered herself into the companion armchair, tasted the coffee and smacked her lips appreciatively. Without the youngsters, without the oldsters, the mood had changed. Brass tacks had been reached, and wishful thinking had been cast aside. There was a rapport between them. Strangely, and despite their differences, there always had been. It was bedded firmly in an appreciation of the other's absolute honesty. Neither jealousy nor envy was there; neither would have changed her life-style for the other's. There could, therefore, *be* honesty and that, of itself, brought an uncommon closeness.

'We'll need help,' said Liz.

'As much as we can get . . . and if possible for free.'

'Rouse?' suggested Liz.

'Who's Rouse?'

'The solicitor. The one who represented William.'

'That's one hell of a recommendation.'

'I think he did his best.'

'Hallelujah!'

'He knows the facts. He has – what d'you call 'em?'

'Depositions?'

'He'll have them.'

'No.' Babs shook her head. 'Not the solicitor.'

'Copies from the lower court from the first hearing . . . surely?'

'Mmm, maybe,' admitted Babs reluctantly. 'But the wig and gown boys screw them up out of recognition.'

'Nevertheless, a basis. Names. Addresses. Somewhere to *start*.'

'Y'know . . .' Babs leaned back in the armchair and held her head on one side. 'That Linley female really impressed you.'

'I believed her,' said Liz simply.

'The question though, eh? Why didn't she do her song and dance act when it could do some good?'

Mary Drever couldn't remember when she'd last been awake at three o'clock in the morning. The clock in the front room had just struck the hour. 'Westminster Chimes'. Bill had been very pig-headed about that. It had to have Westminster Chimes otherwise he wasn't interested. Very nice chimes, too. Very comforting in the darkness when you couldn't sleep. But this was the first time she'd heard the three o'clock strike.

Very dogmatic about everything, Bill. Gas-fired central heating with a Potterton boiler. Nothing less. Potterton or nothing. And with a Horstmann thermostat on every radiator. 'One thermostat in a house means nowt. One for each room. One for each *part* of each room. That means one for each radiator. And Horstmann, and don't try to fob me off with owt less.' Same with everything. Yorkshire stone on the outside. 'Y'see, Mother, it weathers well. It mellows with time. There's nowt bonnier than Yorkshire stone on the outside.' But Cornish stone for the fire surround. Purpose-built; Cornish stone, trimmed and polished;

bronze and red and purple with here and there a glint of 'fool's gold'. And on top – on the roof – Welsh slate. This bungalow. Every timber, every frame, almost every nail and screw, hand-picked. The end-product of a lifetime's experience. The hard-earned knowledge of what was good and what was the best. 'And it's going to be the best, Mother. I don't give a damn what it costs. I cannot abide owt that's not the best.'

Including sons. Including daughters. Only the best and always the best. No back-sliding. No weaknesses ... ever! A hard man to please, but a good husband. But what sort of a father? That was the question.

She stood at the window. The curtains had been drawn back and she could see the glow of lights in the sky from Lessford. Lessford, where the 'bad women' lived. *And* died! Where they'd said William had killed three. 'Their' William. *Her* William. The little lad – the poor bairn – terrified of his father's displeasure. Even when he'd grown up. Even when he'd married. That look in his eyes. The whipped-dog look. And after he'd married. The wrong lass; in a way, an extension of his father; in a way, so like his father that Bill began to loathe her. Funny that. Two people so alike and, because they were so alike, they hated each other. Maybe they could see their own faults in each other. Maybe that. But it hadn't helped William. Poor lad. Poor William.

Beyond the window it was cold. The first, brittle frost of the winter. Ground frost the *Yorkshire Post* had warned ... whatever that meant. Just that it glittered on the grass of the lawn as the light from the full moon caught and reflected its coldness. Not that she was cold. The old-fashioned flannelette nightgown brushed against the radiator and transferred warmth to her body, and the double-glazing kept the real nip beyond the panes.

She wondered ... would William be cold? What sort of bed? What sort of pyjamas? Did they even *allow* pyjamas? Would he be able to sleep? Dreams, maybe? Even nightmares? Poor lad. Silly lad.

Fancy going with women like that. Fancy having a bairn to one, then keeping it to himself. Oh, dear! The daft things men got up to sometimes. No sense of responsibility. Not enough gumption to fill a thimble. Not that it was all *his* fault. When things like that happened the wife was often to blame. Given a good wife a man could keep himself decent. Keep himself respectable. Enough good wives, and women like that would be out of business in no time. No time at all. Given a good wife.

Given a good wife, good parents and a good upbringing.

Behind her back, in the solid, oak-headed double-bed, Bill Drever stirred in his sleep. He ended up on his back and, as he did so, his mouth opened and a steady, gurgling snore came from the back of his throat. Mary Drever turned her head and stared at the hillock of bedclothes under which her husband slept. A good man. A hard worker. A God-fearing man with principles which had never wavered.

A good *father*?

She wondered, and the doubt made her feel guilty ... almost unfaithful.

But what is woman? Only one of
Nature's agreeable blunders.

Who's the Dupe?
Hannah Cowley

'Drever? Drever?'

The cadet rolled the name around his mouth as if he liked the taste of it. He eyed a spider's web at one corner of the cornice, as if seeking inspiration from upon high. He was a thin lad, all bone and bounce and one day – assuming he had the brains to learn good manners and a modicum of humility – he'd make a moderately good copper. For the moment however he was a cadet; long hair, acne and all, and his present templet, as far as police work was concerned, was some cathode-ray cop who *good* weekly left a trail of dead and dying in his wake. He drummed the public counter of Lessford Police Headquarters with his spiky fingers and, for a third time, repeated the name.

'Drever?'

'D.R.E.V.E.R.' said Babs Drever in a dangerously polite voice.

'I know how to spell it,' said the cadet pompously.

'Really? I didn't think you could read.'

The cadet blinked.

Babs snapped, 'It's been in every damn newspaper for weeks. Or do you only read the problems page?'

'Now, look here, miss . . .'

'Don't let the naked fingers throw you, little boy. I've flicked smart-arsed kids like you from my cuffs waiting for *real* men.'

The cadet blushed.

'I want to see the chief constable.'

'Er – I'll have to know why.'

You'll have to know why?

'Yes, miss – ma'am – I shall . . .'

'I'll tell him,' rapped Babs. 'Then if *he* wants you to know, he'll send you a postcard.'

Which was all wrong, of course. Flashy dressed women didn't march into a police headquarters and take over. It wasn't allowed. It wasn't the proper way. This was a police *headquarters*. Not some tin-pot section station. This was where the weight – the *real* weight – hung out. This was where 'they' – as opposed to 'we' – tiptoed around and kept from under everybody's feet. This was . . .

'Sonny.' Babs leaned across the counter. The cadet made as if to back away, but was suddenly aware that his finger-drumming

113

hand was held at the wrist in a grip any judo expert would have been proud of. Bab's voice was on a par with the purr of a wild cat. 'The lesson in cutting down to size is over. Blow. Find me somebody with hair on his chest.'

The fatherly figure, with the chevrons and the new-moon grin on his face, did much to put things right.

'Cadets!' He might have been talking about a badly behaved puppy. 'Blayde himself had more tact.' Babs didn't know who Blayde was, but she let it slide past. The sergeant said, 'Drever? The Drever who got time a couple of days ago?'

'I'm his sister.'

'I see.' The sergeant pushed the tip of his tongue against one cheek. It made him seem to be sucking a gobstopper. 'And according to the lad, you want to see the chief?'

'That's why I'm here.'

The sergeant leaned forward across the counter, and eyed the floor on the public side.

'Where's the petition?' he asked in a friendly enough voice.

'The petition?'

'They all have petitions,' explained the sergeant cheerfully. 'Thousands and thousands of signatures. All saying what sods we are. That, or that British Justice needs its ears syringed.'

Her eyes glinted dangerously. The sergeant held out a hand, as if he was stopping traffic.

'All right. All right. You want to see the chief.'

'I'm *going* to see the . . .'

'But not today. He's in London for a couple of days. One more get-together in the name of crime prevention.' Then before Babs could edge a word in, 'How about one of the officers in charge of the case? Detective Chief Inspector Hoyle?'

'Is he big?' asked Babs suspiciously.

'Big, broad? Big, wide? Big, tall? Big . . .'

'Big, important?'

'*I'm* important,' said the sergeant, without mock-modesty. 'And Hoyle is two pegs up the board from me. *And* C.I.D. . . . which makes him gold-plated.'

Rouse wasn't quite the stick-in-the-mud Liz had expected. A little dusty round the edges, perhaps, but Law – even Criminal

Law – is a dusty subject. By the time a case reaches court all the blood has been hosed away, all the petty hatreds and jealousies have been encapsulated in carefully worded statements, all the high drama has been reduced to simple questions and answers. Thus lawyers tend to be unemotional, musty and, other than in their own company, dreary fellows with which to pass the time of day.

Rouse, however, tried to be different. His office on the third floor had a picture window; admittedly the only view it gave was of a sea of roofs and multitude of chimney pots, but it *was* a picture window. Nothing could hide the yard upon yard of leather-bound volumes, but at least they were neatly shelved and locked away behind glass doors. Clients had a choice of two comfortable armchairs, the desk – only slightly less than a ping-pong table – had a glass top and, among other things, it held a vase of long-stemmed, late-flowering roses. A tray, holding a silver tea service, cups, saucers and a plate of warm, buttered scones had been brought into the office, and ash-trays and a lacquered cigarette box gave silent notice that the nicotine habit was acceptable.

Rouse fingered shredded tobacco from a pouch into the bowl of a stubby pipe. He performed the task slowly, and with obvious joyful anticipation of a pleasure yet to come.

'The Linley girl's mother?' he murmered.

'So she claims.'

'And you believe her?'

'Yes.' Liz didn't hesitate. She tried to put her certainty into the reply. 'It's not wishful thinking. I'm quite sure she's not a crank. Yes, I believe her, absolutely.'

'The question.' Rouse snapped the fasteners of the pouch, blew then sucked at the pipe, then removed it from his mouth, and said, 'Why wait until now?'

'I don't know. I didn't think to ask.'

'An immediate reaction. Some ulterior motive.'

'Another question.' They seemed to be bouncing propositions back and forth between each other. It helped. It cleared the driftwood.

'Why didn't *William* say?'

'Did he know?'

'According to the Linley woman.'

He lighted his pipe, using a hefty brass lighter which was obviously built specifically to light pipes. He tamped the surface of the glowing tobacco with his thumb, re-applied the lighter and puffed clouds of smoke from the corner of his mouth. Having satisfied himself, he dropped the lighter into his jacket pocket, enjoyed a few experimental pulls on the pipe, then removed the pipe from his mouth and held it ready, about six inches from his lips, as the conversation continued.

'He wasn't the most ideal of clients,' he admitted.

'In what way?'

'Honest, but only so far.' He talked in spasms between draws on the pipe. 'He denied the charge. From the first he denied it. Absolutely. But he wouldn't allow an appeal. Even before the verdict. He insisted that if he was convicted, that was that. No appeal. A very unusual attitude to take. If you're innocent, I mean.'

'Was it a good case?' asked Liz. 'I mean, *could* he have been acquitted?'

'With a jury . . . anything.' Rouse grinned ruefully. 'As a case, it was fairly normal. Other than the multiple murder aspect and the mutilations. Circumstantial evidence. But with a murder case, it usually is. Not many murders are actually witnessed. The business of him committing the murders naked. That was a mere argument. A possibility. To explain the absence of bloodstains. But . . .' He sighed. 'An emotive case. "The Copycat Ripper". The old, old story of trial by newspaper. It's a curse we have to live with, I'm afraid. The judge tells the members of the jury they must clear their minds of all pre-conceived ideas. It's a forensic mockery. Who can? The newspapers, television, radio. They do their best. They truly believe they're unbiased. But they're all brainwashed. It's human nature.'

'You say he wasn't an ideal client,' Liz reminded him.

'We had to drag it out of him.' Rouse frowned at the memory. 'He said he hadn't done it. From the first. But . . .' Again the sigh. 'Y'see, Miss Stewart, despite the rantings of a lunatic fringe, the bulk of ordinary people – people who make up an average jury – *want* the police to be right. A man's in the dock. He's already guilty, otherwise he wouldn't be there. Otherwise the police wouldn't *put* him there. As a man-in-the-street – as an ordinary citizen – I can see that attitude. I can even applaud it. But as a lawyer! It turns the presumption of innocence on its head. Technically – theoretically, that is – an accused man needn't open his mouth once he's stated his innocence. He can sit back and watch the Prosecution present its case. Safe in the knowledge that, while the proverbial "element of doubt" remains, he's a free man. But just try it!

'In practice – in the rough and tumble of a court hearing – we have to counter just about every step of the accusation. We *have* to. It's no good a client sitting there on his bum and simply saying "I didn't do it". Your brother-in-law wouldn't accept that. He wouldn't accept that, in practice, we had to prove his innocence just as firmly as the Prosecution had to prove his guilt. We wanted alibis. Alibis . . .' He shook his head in sad disgust. 'All three murders. He was alone in his motor car. Driving. He wouldn't even let us say *where*.'

'Where?' asked Liz quietly.

'This is strictly off the record,' warned Rouse solemnly. 'I shouldn't be telling you. I certainly don't want his wife to know. But in view of what you've told me about the woman who claims to be the Linley girl's mother . . .'

'You have my promise.'

'On his way to Manchester.' The pipe wasn't burning as it should. The lighter was brought into play once more, and he watched her face through the clouds of smoke. He returned the lighter to his pocket and continued, 'All three evenings. At all three times. He was driving to Manchester. Somewhere up on the Pennines. That's not an alibi. That's little more than a joke. It isn't even *that* when we aren't allowed to say *where* he was in his car.'

'Why Manchester?' Liz's face furrowed into a frown of absolute confusion. 'We don't know anybody who lives at Manchester. Or even *near* Manchester.'

'He wouldn't say. Refused point blank. Just that he was in his car. Nothing more.' Rouse hesitated, then added, 'My own guess is a mistress. It happens. Far too often for it to be rare. A married man – a respectable married man – has a piece of fluff tucked away somewhere. He stands accused of a crime. His only alibi to mean anything, is to bring his fancy woman forward to give evidence. He won't – he values his marrige too much – and we can't *make* him.'

'But good heavens,' protested Liz, 'his marriage had gone to pot anyway. Murdering prostitutes! What marriage is going to stand *that*?'

'Don't think we didn't use *that* argument,' sighed Rouse. 'But people get fixed ideas. Your brother-in-law claimed he was innocent. And that was enough for him. If he was acquitted – and I think he truly thought he'd *be* acquitted – it was simply a bad experience. Nothing more. He could pick up his life where he'd left it off.'

'He couldn't,' said Liz gently. 'Not with a seventy-thousand-pound theft charge waiting for him.'

'Oh, that?' The slightly lop-sided, rueful smile added curious charm, and made Rouse look very human. 'I think we could have – er *fixed* that.'

Liz looked surprised.

'Money, Miss Stewart.' the grin grew into a gentle chuckle, then died. 'Embezzlement, that's what it boiled down to. It's bad publicity for any company. They don't like it. Nor do they necessarily want revenge. What they want is their money back. Or as much of it as they can get. Lump sum, or dribs and drabs. They don't care which. Just as long as they break even . . . more or less. We could have worked something out. But once he was convicted – once he went to prison – at that moment, they saw all that money disappearing over the horizon. That's why – who was it? – Jones? . . .'

'Jones.'

'That's why Jones called. To use an expression . . . to "put the bite on".'

'But look . . .' The hope of desperation was in her voice. 'Jones said the firm owned the house, the contents, everything. That William had . . .'

'There's an agreement, Miss Stewart.' Rouse chose his words with great care. 'Jones was over-stating his case a little. A signed agreement. No more than that. Enforceable as a last resort. But – ask yourself the question – what can a firm do with a house and contents? They can't claim *all* the contents. Mrs Drever could fight them. Literally fight them for every stick of furniture. More bad publicity .. which they don't want. And assuming they enforced the agreement, what then? The business of selling. Auctioning. House agent's fees. *My* fee. Again ... more publicity.' The lighter was once more fished from his pocket. More puffing of smoke. More tamping of the tobacco with his thumb. 'A little free advice, Miss Stewart. An offer – any reasonable offer – and they'll jump at it. I'll stake my reputation on that. A second mortgage on the house. A serious talk with your bank manager, and overdraft facilities with the house as collateral. There are ways. I have no doubt – no doubt at all – that your brother-in-law would be agreeable. He'd sign all necessary documents. You can, if you wish – if you go the right way about things – live in that house for the rest of your lives.'

'On tick,' murmured Liz.

'On credit.' Rouse smiled. 'The way a lot of people live, Miss Stewart. Rich people. People who *needn't* live that way. But they use the banks and the building societies. They *use* them. They don't view them as glorified money-boxes. Eventually ...' He moved his shoulders. 'The house will be sold. The furniture will be sold. The debt will be cleared. More than cleared, counting the interest. But meanwhile ... To put it bluntly you – Mrs Drever – won't be around to worry about it.'

It was a solution ... of a sort. Half the problem had been solved ... more or less. Liz felt weight drop from her shoulders. The sheer, blind hopelessnes of the situation was no longer there, thanks to this slightly unusual, down-to-earth solicitor. It was a bonus. Something in addition to what she'd come for and, having lighted a cigarette, she returned to first base and they discussed William, and the Linley woman, and just exactly what might be done in an attempt to save William from his own foolishness.

Rouse was honest to the point of bluntness. 'In a manner of speaking, he's passed the point of no return. Without his permission to appeal, there's little anybody can do.' Nevertheless, Liz pressed on. This was her lucky day. There had to be *something*. Yes, Rouse had a copy of the police file. The case as presented at the lower court. Yes, she could have a complete photostat copy. Today, if she wanted it. He'd have it run through the machine now, and she could take it away with her. The *sub judice* limitation didn't apply. The case was over. Any of the witnesses could be seen and re-questioned at any time. Assuming of course they were *prepared* to be re-questioned.

'What do you hope to achieve?' he asked pleasantly.

'Proof of William's innocence.'

'Even after he's been convicted?' The lop-sided grin, plus the hint that he was humouring her a little.

'It's been done,' she insisted.

'Indeed,' he agreed. 'Erle Stanley Gardner did it scores of times. Unfortunately, Perry Mason died with his creator in 1970.'

'That's not a very nice thing to say.'

'Miss Stewart,' he said somberly, 'I'm not here to be "nice". I'm not even here to be optimistic. I'm here to be *realistic* and, although I wish you luck, I don't think you've a cat in hell's chance.'

Robert and Sal met during the morning break. It was natural and yet there was a shyness. Each knew they'd committed themselves the previous evening, but each wondered whether the other was equally serious.

'Rob.'

'Sal.'

Their fingers touched, as they strolled alongside each other. Sal said, 'About last night . . .'

'It's all right,' muttered Robert.

'No. I mean if you've had second thoughts, that' . . .'

'Second thoughts about what?'

'Y'know. What we . . .'

'Oh! I was wondering if *you'd* had second thoughts.'

'Me?'

'I mean, if . . .'

'No second thoughts, Rob,' she said with unaccustomed timidity.

'That's great. That's super.' And his face illuminated pleasure, as if an electric light bulb had been switched on inside.

Their fingers found each other and without embarrassment they linked hands. Like all first-time lovers with their first-time love they thought they were unique. In the history of the world nobody had ever experienced this breath-stopping surge of unadulterated joy. Scarlett and Rhett were mere bit players. Antony and Cleopatra had walk-on parts. Therefore, in the short time of the morning break, he told her everything. About the Linley woman; what he knew; what Liz had told him. In his enthusiasm he tended to garnish a little, but in the circumstances who could blame him?

Sal said, 'That's great. Dad'll be over the moon.'

'Dad?'

'*My* dad,' then, 'You're coming to tea, Sunday. Parental approval. That sort of thing.'

'Oh ... I couldn't. I ...'

'You *are*.' Her hand squeezed a little. 'Rob, I *want* you to. I want them to know the nice guy I've landed.'

'What – what *about* your father?' A tiny cloud had invaded his clear blue sky.

'Oh, y'know.' She threw it off, like a discarded head-scarf. 'Fuddy-duddies. Not that he's *that* bad. He works in a bank, see? It affects 'em that way. Super-cautious. Not that he is, *really*.'

'Bad blood.' He scowled at the ground. 'I don't blame him. I don't ...'

'Well, I *do*.' Then after the tiny explosion, a happy grin. 'But it doesn't apply now, does it? I mean, *your* father ... Well – he didn't, did he? So it doesn't apply. He'll be pleased. It'll make his day.'

'*Your* father?'

'Yes. And yours, of course.'

'If we can find who did kill them.'

'If we can only find who *did* kill them,' mused Babs. 'That Hoyle character. Oh, very correct. Very polite. He talked for a full hour and said damn-all. Cool but adamant. That about sums it up.'

'I can understand your concern, ma'am. Unfortunately, as far as we're concerned, the case is closed.'

'Yeah. That's what they said about the Dreyfus Case.'

'It's out of our hands. The next step's an Appeal Court, if your brother so decides.'

'Manners!' said Babs indignantly. 'Well dressed. Good looking. On the outside, quite dishy. But inside! I've known refrigerators warmer.'

They'd met up, as arranged, at one of the cafés off Beechwood Brook market square. They sipped tea and exchanged news of their respective successes and failures. Babs, as usual, did most of the talking.

'I asked whether I could see the papers. Christ! You'd have thought I'd asked to try the Turin Shroud for size.'

'That's out of the question, ma'am.'

'Why?'

'They're confidential. Very confidential.'

'Confidential my Aunt Fanny! Everybody not deaf, dumb and blind knows all about the damn case by this time.'

'I can't speak for your Aunt Fanny, ma'm. But I *can* speak about the file. Definitely *not* for public perusal.'

'Funny, with it.' Babs drew hard on her cheroot. A middle-aged woman in a fur coat was sitting at the next table. She screwed up her face and coughed, politely but pointedly. Babs turned her face slightly and blew the smoke through pursed lips directly at the chocolate eclair on its way to the fur-coated woman's mouth. 'Laughing policemen,' she scowled, 'That's all we need to complete the pack.'

'I struck oil.' And if Liz sounded slightly complacent, who could blame her. She lifted the large manilla envelope from alongside the chair, and placed it on the table. She drew out a neatly stapled file, more than half an inch thick. 'What the policeman wouldn't give you,' she said.

'Y'mean?'

'The complete file. A photostat copy.'

'Bingo!'

The fur-coated woman inhaled through quivering nostrils. Her bosom swelled, like a pouter pigeon's breast, but neither Liz nor Babs had time to notice some stranger's outraged indignation.

They ordered fresh tea, pulled their chairs closer together and began reading the copy of the police file. It took more than an hour and the truth was, it was not inspired reading. The language was stilted. The statements (and the statements made up the bulk of the file) were couched in police jargon. Witnesses 'proceeded' rather than 'went'. They 'observed' when in fact they 'saw'.

Fiddling details were emphasised. Times, to the very minute, were included when it was obvious that only an approximation of time could be possible.

Babs drew out her cheeks in disgust and said, 'God! *Z Cars* was never like this. Look, let's concentrate on one. The Linley tart. If we can prove he didn't kill *her*, we're well on the way.'

'If we can come up with who *did* kill her . . .' Liz left the remark unfinished.

So they concentrated their attention upon the Linley killing. The statement of the last person to see her alive; or, at least, the last person prepared to *say* she saw her alive. A certain Olive Laine, who lived in a flat across the landing from Linley's flat. A statement from a certain Peter Rowland Littlejohn, who found her dead body at twenty minutes to midnight. 'Read between the lines, Liz. The bloody pimp, coming to collect his takings.' A statement of identity; Littlejohn again. Statements saying what sort of person she'd been. Words like 'happy', 'carefree' and 'friendly' leapt from the pages; phrases like 'she loved life', 'she was a wonderful companion', 'she was full of vitality'.

Sardonically Babs murmured, 'Evan an out-and-out bag gets a free-issue halo if somebody sticks a knife into her.'

Liz compared statements, then said, 'Five hours. Half-six when Laine saw her alive. Twenty to twelve when she was found. I won't wear *that*.'

'At least half a dozen,' agreed Babs. 'Find 'em. List 'em. Use a pin, but *find* 'em first.'

'So why William? I mean, specifically, why *William*?'

'The first two killings.' Babs leaned sideways and rifled the pages of the file. 'General descriptions of men seen in the vicinity. Could fit anybody. Then at the Linley killing this character – what's his name? – Yardley. Colin Yardley. Claims he saw William leave the building, then drive away in a car. Took the number and make of the car.' More riffling of pages. 'Description fits . . . more or less. Identity parade. Yardley picks William. And that's *it*.' She blew out her cheeks. 'Christ, I wouldn't hang a cat on *that* evidence.'

'We're biased.'

'Biased, be damned! No fingerprints . . .'

'Smudged, according to the report.'

'No blood group . . .'

'There *wasn't* any blood. According to the police . . .'

'And *that's* fixing the question, once you've come up with some sort of crappy answer, if ever I saw it. All this nature-boy baloney. Your solicitor's right. William's short on marbles. He could have walked away from this without even half trying, if he'd only let his lawyers off a leash.'

'And that leaves . . .' Liz leaned back in her chair, tasted cold tea, pulled a face, then lighted a cigarette. 'That leaves the woman who claims to be Linley's mother. Who claims William is Linley's father.'

'You believe her,' Babs reminded.

'I *believed* her. I'm starting to have doubts.'

'I would,' said Babs grimly, 'like to meet that torturous bitch.'

'You will. You probably will . . . eventually.'

There was a period of quiet. A period in which frustration, almost amounting to defeat, brought on a feeling of futility. What had they expected? The solid, down-to-earth Liz? The in-there-with-both-feet-and-screw-the-opposition Babs? What *had* they expected? In the silence, they each asked themselves that question. The police files had seemed the key with which to unlock all doors but (as any copper could have told them) police files are not built up to create confidence in people whose aim it is to prove a convicted murderer innocent. Two amateurs were out to make the professionals look foolish. That, stripped of all the glitter, was what it was all about. The name of the ballgame. And as Rouse had remarked, they hadn't a cat in hell's chance.

'Dammit, hand me that file.' Babs stirred herself and reached across for the sheaf of papers. 'This creep Yardley. Forget the identity parade for a second. He claims he saw William leave the block of flats. Saw him drive away in a car. Took the make and number of the car. *Why the hell should he*?'

Liz sat up and showed interest.

Babs stabbed the place in the file with an indignant finger. 'No reason given *why* he was interested in the car. *Why* he was interested in whoever came out of the block of flats. A whole block of flats. He could have lived there. He could have been visiting. So why? Why notice him? Why remember the car number? It stinks.' She dropped the file onto the table, and some of the frustration melted, as she said, 'Friend Yardley is our first port of call. And this time *I'm* the doubting Thomas he has to convince.'

It was Friday, therefore it was 'Baking Day'. Part of the pattern of the week; every week since they were married . . . and before. Not bread any more. Bread was hard work and time consuming, and they'd found a tiny, one-man bakery where the bread and 'oven-bottom-cakes' met even Bill's high standard. Nevertheless Friday was 'Baking Day' and habits of a lifetime couldn't be completely broken. The tarts and the buns, the cinnamon cake and the fruit pies. The weekly supply was made on a Friday and, as long as she was able, would continue to be made on a Friday. Her gnarled fingers weren't as nimble as they'd once been, but the know-how was there. She didn't have to concentrate. She didn't even have to think about what she was doing. Like riding a bike. Like swimming. Get the hang, do it enough times, the knack never leaves you. Even the measuring of the ingredients. The scales were merely a tool to be used; she measured by cup or by spoon, and the scales simply verified her own expertise.

The kitchen was warm from the oven. Warm and cosy and her domain. The one room in the bungalow where she had the last say. The oven, for instance. Bill had wanted one of the latest fancy ovens; clocks and timing devices; spits and rotisseries. She'd wanted none of it. Plain rings, a plain grill and an oven *she* controlled. All she'd ever wanted. All she'd ever wished for. She could have asked for more. A lot more. But being greedy – well . . .

The inner door opened and Bill Drever wandered into the kitchen. He was on edge. Retirement didn't suit him and since William . . .

He tried to be jovial and said, 'Smells good, Mother.'

She dusted flour from her hands onto the baking-board, but didn't answer.

'There's nobody can cook like you. Nobody can bake fruit pies just the way I like . . .

'The way to a man's heart,' she said flatly.

'Aye. And it's a fact.'

'If only a full belly was *all* it needed,' she said softly. And, with bitterness which wasn't hidden.

'Summat troubling you?' he asked.

'Oh, no.' The sarcasm was heavy because she wasn't used to being sarcastic. 'What have *I* to be troubled about?'

'Hey, Mother. Let's not . . .'

'*Don't!*' It was a soft scream. Intense. Almost hysterical. In a calmer voice she said, 'Don't ever call me "mother" again. I don't deserve it.'

'Nay, be damned . . .'

'A son and a daughter, and I've stood by and let *this* happen to them.'

'You can't blame yourself for what . . .'

'Not just *me*.' And it was well past tears. A hard, dry misery, far deeper, far more painful than the misery of weeping. In a tone he'd never heard before she said, 'You slept well last night.'

'I slept,' he agreed.

'I didn't. I *couldn't*.'

'You should have wakened me. I'd have . . .'

'The one person I could do without.'

'Eh?' he gasped.

'Bill Drever.' Her voice was hoarse but steady. 'I never thought I'd live to see the day. I'd give anything – anything . . .' She stopped, swallowed, then said, 'If I was thirty years younger I'd walk out of this *bloody* bungalow, and you'd never clap eyes on me again. Now . . . get out of my kitchen.'

Carol had to be seen. Bryant had put it in a nutshell. 'The one thing she mustn't feel is alone. Unwanted. What she did had had its roots in self-pity.' Babs had put it more pithily. 'She's your sister, okay. But catch *me* doing a thing like that because of something in pants. I'd spit in his eye first. But, y'know, she needs her tiny hand holding, I guess.'

Therefore by common consent Liz visited the hospital that Friday afternoon. It was a duty, but she tried to act it out as a pleasure. The grapes and the box of glacé fruits were received with a wan smile and a muttered word of thanks. The still-bandaged wrist was in full view on top of the coverlet. There was a touch of make-up on the lips, but beyond that nothing. The 'second phase', as Bryant had called it, was well under way.

'Shame, covered up by Victorian melodrama stuff. But have patience. Play along with it. It'll pass.'

The sickly smile returned and Carol said, 'I'll never be able to repay you. Any of you.'

'Fiddlesticks. That's what elder sisters are for.'

'You *say* that, but . . .'

'Good news.' Liz interrupted the performance with a deliberately bright and breezy tone. She pulled a chair nearer to the bed, and said, 'Rouse . . . the solicitor. That seventy-thousand debt thing. It can be handled.'

'I can't see how on earth . . .'

'Get yourself out of here. Put all this behind you. Then, between us, we can gradually write it off.'

She told of her talk with Rouse; exaggerating a little, minimizing the difficulties, over-enthusing the possibilities and making them sound like mere inconveniences not big enough to slow down, much less halt, the eventual way out of the wood. It was hard work, not least because Carol didn't *want* to believe. Nothing was said or even hinted about Ruth Linley or the probability that William was innocent. Again Bryant's advice. 'Leave her something to hang onto. Something – somebody – to blame. Her husband, if you like. In a manner of speaking, she's drowning. Part of her even *wants* to drown. So leave her one spar to cling onto, otherwise she might go down.'

Liz found her facial muscles cramping a little. The fixed smile wasn't part of her normal self. Nor was the fussing; the straightening of the bedclothes, the unwrapping of the glacé fruits, the fiddling with the bits and pieces on the bedside locker. But the time had to be filled, and nothing less than an hour seemed reasonable. They talked of Robert, they talked of Anne, they even talked of Babs, but this was a dangerous subject, and called for some quick footwork.

'I think she could have come up before now.'

'She's been busy. Schedules. Things like that.'

'Her own brother.'

'She – er – she's taking it harder than you might think,' lied Liz.

'Why didn't she come with you?'

'Anne and Robert.' Liz fished around for some reasonable

excuse. 'They have appetites. College. And Anne's gone in to work. Somebody had to stay at home to make a meal.' Then, because that sounded a weak reason, 'And her parents, of course. She has to – y'know – if she can find time I think she'd like to visit them.'

A visit of disjointed sentences on the one hand, and on the other an almost childlike petulance. It was hard going and after an hour Liz was pleased to make excuses to leave.

Bryant was waiting. Liz found herself wondering when the hell he found time to minister to his own patients, and whether he was on full-time duty at Beechwood Brook Cottage Hospital, then immediately felt guilty at having such thoughts.

'How's the lassie?' he asked.

'Oh – er – fine.'

'She's getting better.' He chuckled. 'She created a little this morning because her egg was hard boiled. It's a good sign.'

Liz smiled.

'I was – er – wondering.' Bryant measured his stride with hers, and they walked slowly down the corridor. 'D'you like ballet?'

'Ballet?'

'Y'know ... ballet?'

'Well, I ...' The unexpectedness of the question had caught her completely off balance. 'Yes, of course I like ballet. When it's on television, I always ...'

'No, I mean the real thing.'

'I've never *seen* the real thing. Out here in the provinces we don't often ...'

'Lessford Opera House.' He sounded like a man taking a cold plunge. In there, over the head, in order to shorten the agony. 'The Scottish Ballet Company. Cinderella. I – er – I have two tickets.'

'Oh!'

'We could make an evening of it. I'd pick you up then a meal afterwards.'

'I really don't think ...'

'No strings,' he added hastily. 'Don't get wrong ideas. Just the theatre, a meal, then home.'

'W-when?' Her equilibrium hadn't quite recovered. 'I mean which ...'

'This evening.'

'Oh, I couldn't. I have things to . . .'

'I know. You have to wash your hair. Rinse out your undies. All the other piffling excuses women make when they don't want to be rude and say "No".' He sounded suddenly angry; angry at himself for making a fool of himself. 'I'm sorry I . . .'

'No!' she gasped. 'Not that. Really.' She bit at her lower lip for a moment then blurted, 'I'll come. I'd love to come.'

He blew out his cheeks, then took a deep breath. The anger went as swiftly as it had come, and he smiled and said, 'You have no idea. Asking you. God!'

'As bad as that?'

'Amputations are easy by comparison. But – y'know – thanks.'

'What – what time?' Now she was slightly embarrassed.

'I'll pick you up at six. That okay?'

'Fine. And thank you.'

'You'll love it,' he promised. 'Ballet on the box isn't *real* ballet. Like war movies. Not remotely like the real thing.'

She walked home, and as she walked her emotions seemed to be swirling around an electric mixer. Happiness; that was there and kept popping up to the surface and blanketing all other feelings for the moment. But guilt was there in almost equal measure. William wrongly convicted . . . and she was going to the ballet. Carol recovering from an attempt at taking her own life . . . and she was going to the ballet. Babs badgering away trying to unearth proof of William's innocence . . . and she was going to the ballet. And Anne, and Robert, and *everything* . . . and *she* was going to the ballet. It was wrong, but it was wonderful. She shouldn't have accepted, but she was going to have a marvellous time. She was being monumentally disloyal, but already she was looking forward to it like a child anticipating Christmas.

Snout was still around. The impression was he'd kicked the sleeping habit and that he could also get along fine without food. His baggy eyes were a little baggier, tiny creases etched webs along the surface of his podgy face and the beginnings of a beard shadowed his jowls and his multiple chins. But he was still around.

His two companions were on the verge of revolt.

'Nothing's going to happen,' wailed the photographer.

Snout ignored the remark.

The cub reporter said, 'Snout, this time it's a complete bum. Why can't you accept it?'

'Seen the wife lately?' gurgled Snout.

'I'm not married. How the hell . . .'

'*The* wife. Drever's wife, you gormless cretin.'

'I thought you said . . .'

'In an ambulance at a guess.' Snout enjoyed a phlegmy chuckle. 'Whatever, I want to be here to ask questions.'

'No mercy,' muttered the photographer.

'None whatever, laddie.' The chuckle died and was replaced by a scowl. 'Like Drever when he knifed the scrubbers.'

'Friends of yours?' asked the photographer sarcastically.

'I have no friends. That's why I'm good.' Snout knew his worth, and modesty was not one of his faults. Then to the cub reporter. 'Worth remembering, sonny. Sod friendship. Top people don't *have* friends. It's a luxury only slobs can afford.'

It quietened them for the moment. They hated him. They despised him. But as fellow-professionals they recognised the 'great' as opposed to the 'good'. The man without feelings could produce copy denied to more humane reporters. The public might be aghast, but they'd queue up to buy it and read it. The Press Council might rant, but once it was in print the circulation stayed high. Fellow-journalists might sneer, but secretly they'd give their eye-teeth to parallel the scoop. Forget the N.U.J. Code of Conduct; it could be stretched and bent to by-pass just about everything. Just the story, boy. Just dig deeper than the surface dirt and find the *real* slime.

good! Daylight was drooping its eyelids into the dusk, and Snout and his two buddies stood guard upon the gate. The car drew to a halt, parked, and Babs climbed from the driving seat and locked the door. She stopped directly in front of Snout and gazed up into his sneering face.

'You still around, fat man?' she said coldly.

Snout moved his head in a single nod.

'How long?' asked Babs.

'Who knows?'

'You're a louse, y'know that?'

'So I've heard.' Snout remained unperturbed.

'Just to remind you.' She stared in turn at the other two. 'Three of you. Three lice. Three snot-nosed examples of what it's like to be a disgrace to the human race.'

She turned and strode towards the house.

The photographer said, 'That does it.'

'What?' Snout looked mildly surprised.

'That's me finished, Snout. Too damn right, that's what we are. I may be dumb, but I know when I've out-stayed my welcome.'

'Me too.' All it needed was a lead. The young reporter stood alongside the photographer. 'You're on your own, Snout. I won't even wish you luck.'

They left and, other than a contemptuous curl of the lips, Snout did nothing to hinder or discourage their departure. He was the boy. He was the lad. And, come sometime, the exclusive he could sniff in the air would be his for the taking.

It was cold on the Tops. Cold and growing dark. And very lonely. The environment matched Bill Drever's mood. He'd driven to the Tops, parked the car and started walking. From nowhere to nowhere. Just walking; keeping his limbs moving in time with his thoughts.

Mary – *his* Mary – and all these years she'd kept her true feelings locked away. Dammit that wasn't right. That wasn't fair. It wasn't what marriage was about in any shape or form. He thought the world of her. He wasn't a demonstrative man, it wasn't his nature, but dammit she shouldn't have to be told. She should *know*. He wouldn't have wed her else.

Funny. Bloody women . . . queer cattle, all. Even Mary. Never able to understand. Nearly half a century they'd been man and wife, and she *still* had daft ideas. She was pushing the years behind her. All right. Who the hell wasn't? Who the hell *didn't* feel their age? But she couldn't understand. She wasn't old to him. Not through his eyes. She wasn't even middle-aged. When *he* looked at her he saw the bright-eyed lass he'd stood at the altar with. The same bonny lass. The same age, the same everything. 'Growing old together' *meant* that, if it meant owt. It meant you were too close to see the age. Too close. Too near. What you felt,

131

you saw. And if you didn't talk about it, that didn't mean it wasn't there. Lovey-dovey stuff wasn't up his street. But by God he *felt* it.

And now all this talk about 'if I was thirty years younger'.

Nay, lass, be fair. Be decent. I've tried. I've tried bloody hard. Don't blame me . . . not all of it. Hot-headed I might have been sometimes. Hot-headed and short-tempered. And – all right – happen the bairns *were* a bit frightened sometimes. Happen. But I was never deliberately cruel. Never meant to hurt. My own bairns! Nay, lass. Be fair. If I frightened 'em, you should have told 'em. Hot-headed, short-tempered, but as far as my own family was concerned, all wind and piss. You *knew* that. You had to know *that*. Dammit, I'd have torn a limb off for either of 'em. William or Barbara. Stick and lift and they could have had the very blood from my veins, but I just couldn't *tell* 'em.

That I'll admit. That much I'll admit and not even try to excuse. I don't have the gift of tongue. Never have had. Even when we were courting . . . *you* knew. I didn't have to go in for daft talk. I didn't have to keep *telling* you. Dammit, you *knew*. Why, in God's name, didn't you tell *them*? It was no less pure. No less real. You knew what I thought about you. I thought as much about them. Still do. *Still do*!

Mary, luv. Mary, my bonny. 'If I was thirty years younger . . .' Say it, my luv, if you must. Say it, but don't mean it. For God's sake, don't *mean* it. Never *mean* it. Owt but that . . .

Babs was strangely calm about it. Almost, it seemed, relieved. 'Oh, good. Good. A spot of culture. It'll set us up for the week.' Which in view of the fact that her intended 'talk' with the witness, Yardley, hadn't materialised, was a little odd. In some curious, back-to-front way slightly offensive; as if, secretly, she was rather glad that Liz wouldn't be there.

'He's a plumber,' she explained. 'Out on a site somewhere. I've fixed up to see him this evening.'

'In that case, I can cancel the trip to the . . .'

'No, no.' Babs waved the smoked salmon sandwich in an airy gesture of dismissal. That was Babs for you. Over the eyes in debt, but she'd bought sliced smoked salmon for a sandwich snack before Robert and Anne arrived home. It was nice though.

Liz couldn't remember enjoying a scratch meal as much. There was a sort of schoolgirl-tuckshop atmosphere in the kitchen. Babs said, 'His wife – there's a flash piece for you – in the amateur operatic crowd. There's a rehearsal tonight. Yardley trots along to help shift the scenery or something.'

'I really think I should . . .'

'Liz, darling. I'm not going naked. I've recruited old po-face into the ranks.'

'Old – er – po-face?'

'Hoyle. That slightly dishy detective gentleman who wouldn't play ball this morning.'

'Oh!'

'Off-duty of course. But Yardley won't know that.'

'Are policemen ever off duty?' asked Liz weakly.

'He'll come *on* duty with a rush if I strike oil,' promised Babs.

They enjoyed the sandwiches in silence for a few minutes. Lush, flaky smoked salmon, with fresh butter and brown bread cut into thin, ladylike slices. And freshly ground coffee, newly percolated. Liz found herself thinking she could handle this life-style very easily. No sweat. The way Babs lived. No real worries. No hassle. Just take the goodies and don't ask 'How' too many times. It was one way. Maybe the best way in the long term.

'How did you do it?' she asked at last.

'Eh?'

'Hoyle. This morning he was very . . .'

'Oh, that was this *morning*.' Babs looked surprised that the obvious *wasn't* obvious. 'I've worked out his wavelength since then. I just walked in on him and asked, that's all.'

'Asked?' Liz was still mystified.

'Well, y'know, in a way. The serious ones. It's like taking pennies from a blind man's tray. The tricky types are the ones to be wary of.'

'All worked out.' Liz shook her head. Part bewilderment. Part criticism. Part envy. 'The whole of life. Easy when you know how.'

'Honey.' Babs might have been a mother imparting wisdom to a slightly backward child. 'We come from a hole, we finish in a hole. The middle bit .. that's up to us. Hard or easy. It's a very simple choice. You chew it or you spit it out. Me? I'm only interested in the tasty pieces.'

Bill Drever didn't know how to apologise. That was his trouble, although he didn't recognise it. Just saying sorry. He couldn't do it, because his whole life had been built upon the premise that 'being sorry's no damn good; you shouldn't have done it that way in the first place'. Which was fine when it applied to some stupid mistake made by a bricklayer or a joiner or a plasterer, but when it applied to human relationships it was a non-starter. Come to that he couldn't see what the hell he had to be sorry *about*. That was the Catch 22 part. He knew he *was* sorry, but for the life of him he couldn't work out *why* he was sorry. Just that it was something terrible. Something beyond his comprehension. Something he could never mend.

He parked his car in the drive – didn't bother to garage it – then hesitantly, almost timidly, entered his own home, his own living room. He closed the door gently, then stood there watching her. In the armchair. Fingers twisted on her lap. Head lowered. Eyes red from recent weeping. Iron-grey hair awry.

Twice he tried to speak, but the words wouldn't come. A dry throat, parched lips and the simple fact that he didn't know what to say.

Then he croaked, 'You wouldn't, would you, lass?'

She looked up startled. Not by the words, but by the helpless pleading quality in the tone. Something she'd never heard before. Something she never expected to hear.

'Even – y'know if you *were* thirty years younger?' he whispered. He stammered, 'What I've done. I dunno. Honest, lass, I *don't* know. Whatever . . . I didn't mean it. I wouldn't hurt you, lass. Not you. Not the bairns. Not . . .'

Then he choked and clamped his teeth tight, but his face folded and the tears spilled from his eyes, and he began to shake his head from side to side. Slowly and in complete perplexity. The great bore of unaccustomed emotion seemed to be tearing him apart. He was unable to cope, unable to understand, unable to put into words a fraction of what he was feeling.

She stood up from the chair. Steady, despite the arthritic joints and the hammering of age and recent events. And now *she* was the strong one, and this husband of hers – this husband she'd verbally rejected only hours before – was a child, her child, who required above all else her comforting. She walked to him, put her arm across his shoulders and kissed his wet cheek.

'Nay, lad,' she said gently, 'we all say things. We don't mean them.' She led him slowly to the chair. 'Sit down, luv. Dry thy eyes, light thy pipe. How could *I* ever leave *thee*?' She waited while, still sobbing, still shaking his head, he lowered himself into the chair. She touched the top of his head with her lips and said, 'I'll brew some tea. Apple pie ... you like apple pie. Tha knows.' She smiled. 'We say things. We *all* say things. We shouldn't, but we do.'

Lessford Opera House was a theatre. A *real* theatre; what the Victorians who had built it *expected* a theatre to be like. Red plush, gold paint, cherubs and chandeliers; orchestra stalls, pit, circle and balcony. The lot. An evening at Lessford Opera House meant something. Not, perhaps, as much as it had once meant: the greats; Little Tich, Harry Champion, Nellie Wallace, Harry Tate, Houdini, the Houston Sisters and a grand parade of others of a like stature had graced its massive stage; but even today it put on the shows and pulled in the crowds. It was the best and biggest provincial theatre for miles around. At Christmas it staged an annual pantomime magnificent enough to merit bus and train excursions. It had no gimmicks, other than its own brand of excellence and the fact that it still retained that almost lost 'feel' of the theatre; the hush as the house lights dimmed, and that glorious anticipation of entertainment at its best as the great curtains parted to reveal the culmination of a dozen or more art forms, all interwoven to create the peculiar magic of 'the theatre' in its various guises.

Looking down from the front row of the circle, Liz could see that the first three rows of the orchestra stalls had been removed in order to provide sitting and stand space for what amounted to a symphony orchestra. The barrier around the orchestra pit had also been removed, and it was patently obvious the Scottish Ballet Company meant to be heard as well as seen.

Bryant said, 'Comfy?'

Liz nursed the box of chocolates and the programme, smiled and said, 'Marvellous. This is really marvellous.'

Nor was it less than the truth. During the drive to Lessford the ice had been broken. 'Look, you can't keep calling me "doctor" all the time. I might forget myself and whip your tonsils out and that wouldn't do. Peter. D'you mind?' 'Liz.' And that had been it. With the ease of a hand slipping into a glove they'd slipped into first-name friendship.

They stood up to allow three newly-arrived members of the audience to pass and, as they settled into their seats once more, Liz said, 'I expected Prokofiev.'

'Oh, no.' He grinned, and she suddenly realised that he was a dedicated music buff. 'The Old Cinderella story. *Zolushka*, that's Prokofiev's version. Then there's Massenet's *Cendillon* and Wolf-Ferrari's *Cenerentola*. But this is Rossini's stab at it. *La Cenerentola*. Originally meant to be an opera, but don't let that fool you. And of course the Scottish Opera boys and girls give it its English name. Cinderella. Very down to earth our haggis-eating brethren. *And* rattling good dancers and musicians.'

She matched grin for grin, and wanted to release a gurgle of happy laughter. The atmosphere was getting at her. The members of the orchestra edging their way to their places. Programme sellers guiding newcomers down the aisles. The soft hub-bub of conversation with, in the background, the oboe giving a soft 'A' and the strings easing in on it, then rippling through finger-flexing runs. Like a field of international runners limbering up for the start of a great race. As exciting, as breath-holding as that. Then the conductor mounted the rostrum, tapped his music stand, then raised his baton. And the runners lined up and held themselves tense and ready for the start-gun.

The dust in the church hall irritated the nostrils. The whole damn place was fusty and dry. Walk across the lino-covered stage and you left footmarks. Touch the drapes and a thin cloud of grey was released into the air.

Babs murmured, 'Jesus wept! Talk about cleanliness coming after Godliness.'

Hoyle grunted and for the moment kept his opinions to himself. David Hoyle. Detective chief inspector. A man with a great future ahead of him and also who was aware of that fact. He was immodest enough to recognise himself as a born thief-taker, but conscious of the necessity to hone that natural ability to an edge sharp enough to carve a way to the top. But for all that, a man of inbuilt compassion, and moreover a man not quite sure of himself. Married to a PhD, he worried away, terrier-like, at subjects only marginally connected with law-enforcement, and sometimes not at all connected, in a never-ending attempt, not so much to drag himself up to the level of intelligence of his wife, but rather to make sure that *he* didn't drag *her* to a lower standard by not being able to either talk with her, or understand her quicksilver mental ability. The result was a curious mix of confidence and doubt. And (contrary to what Babs liked to believe) the doubt had brought him, off duty, to this dingy church hall where the witness Yardley's wife was rehearsing a lead part in *The Gondoliers* while Yardley himself worked as general dogsbody behind the scenes.

Yardley was a small, dark-skinned man, on the verge of going bald and with darting, suspicious eyes. He cared not one jot about music, but his wife, a one-time local beauty queen, still had a smart eye for the romantically inclined bloods of the amateur operatic society. Yardley, therefore, scene-shifted – did what he was told to do – knowing that while *he* was there she might flirt a little, actress-fashion, but his very presence prevented anything more serious than an extension of the play-acting which took place on the creaking stage.

He saw Hoyle and Babs approaching along the body of the hall, and his quick, worried scowl gave Babs hope and Hoyle concern. On stage Gianetta (née Mrs Yardley) warbled 'Thank you, gallant *gondolieri*! In a set and formal measure it is scarcely necesary to express our pleasure,' to the accompaniment of a very metallic, slightly out-of-tune piano. A bearded young man, wearing pebble-lens spectacles interrupted the proceedings by bawling from the stage apron, 'Look, love. You're supposed to be shy, see? Don't do the calf-eye routine. Play it straight it'll come across funnier.' The singer pouted her temporary displeasure, then turned to the pianist and said, 'Four in, Fred. Then take it from "Listen to him! Well, I never!".' '*Three* in,' corrected Fred, and the bespectacled young man added, '*Three* in, darling. And no business this time.'

Yardley left his place at one side of the stage, and wandered forward to meet them. Before they spoke the three of them strolled, almost off-handedly, to the semi-privacy of a row of wooden chairs which lined one side of the hall.

'The wife told me.' Yardley spoke first.

'A matter of verification,' said Hoyle quietly. 'You don't mind?'

'Why should I?'

The impression was that Yardley was already on the defensive. The sullen expression, the slightly-too-quick counter-question, the shift of the eyes from Hoyle to Babs, then back to Hoyle again.

'To get it right,' said Hoyle. He unfolded a quarto sheet which he'd taken from an inside pocket. He recited times and places descriptions and car numbers, then said, 'That how it was?'

'I gave evidence. I don't lie on oath.'

'This club.' Babs spoke for the first time. 'The – er – what is it?'

'Lessford Bridge Club.'

'But you weren't at the club. Not *inside* the club.'

'Does she . . .' began Yardley.

'She's with me.' It was no less than the truth, but Hoyle managed to make it sound as if Babs was a member of the force. 'Just answer the question.'

'I was dummy,' said Yardley in a low voice. 'They tend to smoke too much. I wanted a breath of clean air.'

'A walk?' suggested Babs.

'Bit of a stroll. Not far.'

'But far enough to pass the block of flats?'

'Obviously. I saw Drever leave.'

'You knew it was Drever?'

'Of course.'

'How far?' asked Hoyle. He was the professional and knew that Babs was pushing the questioning along much too quickly. 'How far from the club to the flats? We didn't establish the distance.'

'A hundred yards, more or less.'

'Going or coming?'

'Eh?'

'Going from the club or coming back to the club?'

'Er . . . coming back, I think. Yes, I'd just about turned round to stroll back when . . .'

'A dummy hand?' interrupted Babs.

'Yes.' Yardley turned to Hoyle and snapped, 'Look why the hell is she . . .'

'Answer the lady's questions, please,' drawled Hoyle.

Yardley made as if he was going to argue, changed his mind, then turned and glowered at Babs.

'Slower than chess,' observed Babs pointedly.

'Eh?'

'Leaving the club. Going for a two hundred yard stroll . . .'

'*One* hundred yards. Don't . . .'

'There and back, buster.'

'Oh!'

'And spotting Drever?'

'Yes.' He nodded. 'I've already . . .'

'What was he doing?'

'Leaving the building. The flats. He was . . .'

'How the . . .' began Babs.

Hoyle cut in, 'Remind us, Mr Yardley. Was he running? Hurrying?'

'No. Just – y'know – leaving.'

'What attracted your attention?'

'Well, y'know, the two previous killings. The description of the man the police wanted to . . .'

'It gave his height. It gave his build. It gave his approximate age. That's about all.' Hoyles swivelled his head slowly. 'Four men here, in this room, it could have fitted any of the four.'

On the stage a red-faced, roly-poly man with a drooping moustache bawled, 'That celebrated, cultivated, underrated nobleman, The Duke of Plaza-Toro!'

In the beginning before the curtains parted, Liz had she been asked would have admitted to a 'liking' of the works of Gioacchino Rossini. A liking, but not much more than that. Nice music. Music with dash and excitement. Overtures like *The Silken Ladder, The Thieving Magpie, William Tell.* Brass-band-in-the-park music, evoking memories of warm summer evenings and deck-chairs and dancing, sometimes even noisy sound. Typical whoopee Italian stuff.

That in the beginning . . .

The ballet dancers were great, but she'd expected them to be great. What she hadn't expected was the music. The shear magnificence of that ballet music from Cinderella, played by a top-drawer orchestra, stunned her into open-mouthed wonder. Climax after climax belted her back into her seat. The soft passages wept as only fine instruments picking the notes from a great score can weep.

There was an interval and Bryant said, 'You haven't touched your sweeties. You haven't even opened the box.'

'I can't believe it,' she gasped softly.

'What's that?'

'Rossini. You know, *Rossini*.'

'Lassie.' Bryant laughed softly. 'You're not the first. Why do you think Verdi dedicated his *Requiem Mass* to him? *He* knew. One superb composer acknowledging the stature of another.'

On stage Mrs Yardley sang, 'Kind sir, you cannot have the heart our lives to part . . .'

Off stage Mr Yardley said, 'What the hell am I supposed to have done?'

'Lied a little?' suggested Babs sweetly.

'Made a mistake,' said Hoyle hurriedly. 'We all make mistakes, Yardley. You're only human.'

'When you were after Drever you didn't . . .'

'We were never "after" any one individual.' Hoyle's voice hardened. 'We don't work that way. We were "after" the truth. This is a verification. A double-check if you like. That we *found* the truth.'

Hoyle was patently unhappy. Yardley was equally patently worried. As far as Babs was concerned it boiled down to a grim satisfaction. But although they talked for more than an hour, the sum total was merely the strengthening of a doubt. Once a fortnight Yardley visited his club. He played bridge with fellow-members. He was a non-smoker, therefore when he was 'dummy' he often took the opportunity to breathe fresh air. Other members did the same. He'd seen this man leave the block of flats. Was he hurrying? No. Did he look scared? No. Was there *anything* about him to attract attention? No. Just that with the

'Copycat Ripper' stories fresh in the news, everbody was keeping their eyes skinned. He saw the man climb into a car and noted the make and the number of the car. Why? Well, that was part of keeping your eyes skinned, wasn't it? But (and back to the original problem) why *that* man and why *that* car? Good God, the police had asked for public co-operation, hadn't they? They'd appealed for any assistance likely to lead them to the murderer. He'd only done what the police had *asked* people to do. And now having performed his public duty, *and* after the man had been convicted, he was being harassed. In a roundabout way he was being called a liar. The hell he'd help the police again. The hell he'd do *anything* to assist the police in future.

As Babs and Hoyle walked from the hall Mrs Yardley was singing, 'If you do what you ought not to, do they give the usual warning?'

Later that evening two conversations took place. Their respective locations were miles apart, but in one respect their main subject-matter was similar. The trial and conviction of William Archibald Drever, and the emotional ripples it had caused to so many lives.

Robert and Anne had already gone to bed. Liz and Babs were once more in the kitchen. They were sipping hot chocolate, smoking cigarettes and, once again, talking the day's events to a close.

'Peter says Carol should be home tomorrow.'

'*Peter*!' Bab's smile bordered upon the lewd.

Liz coloured and said, 'He's given me a wonderful evening.'

'Nice going, kid.'

'Not *that* way, you – you . . .'

'Slut?' The smile broadened and lost its suggestiveness. '*Any* way, honey. If anybody deserves it . . .'

'Tell me what happened with Yardley,' interrupted Liz. 'Everything.'

'He's a fink.' Babs drew on her cheroot. 'He's a frightened fink. He's also a liar.'

'You mean . . .'

'Just that, my pet.' She sighed and pulled a wry face. 'My policeman chum did his best, but brother William is safely caged and that leaves Yardley frightened, but not frightened enough.'

'Damn,' muttered Liz.

'Yeah, damn. *And* blast. *And* set fire to it. But if you recall I said we hadn't a hope in hell.'

Pat and David Oldfield were in night clothes and dresing-gowns. Theirs was a well-regulated life; a life with a simple, uncomplicated pattern and part of that pattern was this before-bed period, when Pat sat on the sheepskin rug at David's feet before the dying embers of the open fire. Her head resting against David's knees while she smoked the last cigarette of the day. David sipping at the hot toddy and occasionally stroking her hair. That they were approaching middle-age meant nothing. This last part of each day was their private world, with no secrets and a silent release of love for each other which was too deep for words and the most precious thing they possessed.

David murmured, 'This thing between Sal and the Drever boy.'

'He isn't a boy, darling. Their generation. At eighteen he isn't a boy.'

'Sal's still a child.'

'*Our* child.'

'Pat, my sweet, don't think I don't know how lucky I am. How lucky we *both* are. But *our* child.'

'You worry,' she smiled, but it wasn't a criticism.

'I worry,' agreed softly. He tasted his drink. 'I worry because I don't want anything to break.'

She knew what he meant, and because she knew and knew that this too was part of her reason for loving him, her silence spoke far more than words.

'Have you met him?' he asked.

'No.'

'Pity.'

'Why?'

'I'd trust your judgement, that's all.'

'What about Sal's judgement?' she asked gently.

He sighed, but didn't reply.

'I wish we were in *my* part of the world,' said Babs grimly.

'Eh?' Liz didn't understand.

'Friend Yardley. I know people – not friends but I know them – *they'd* make him talk.'

'Babs!'

'And why not? They'd string him up by the thumbs – by the balls if necessary – but we'd get the truth.'

'I didn't know you . . .' Liz closed her mouth.

'Mixed in that sort of company?' Babs drew on the cheroot, exhaled, then tasted hot chocolate. 'Television – especially documentaries – necessitates crawling along a few drains sometimes. You tend to meet some of the rats. All the King Rats have a yen for glamour. They think the box – anybody, anything associated with the box – gives 'em it.'

'But they're not your *friends*?' There was real anxiety in the question.

'I *use* people,' said Babs bluntly. Grimly. 'Down there in the Big City that's the way things work. I use them, they use me. In my world it's all top shine. Only the bastards survive, and I'm a survivor.'

'You're selling yourself short,' smiled Liz. 'You're . . .'

'Don't take me at face value, honey.' There was a strange seriousness, a strange bitterness, in her tone. 'If it's necessary to be a bitch, I'll be a bitch. Anywhere. Any day. Any way that's needed. I don't give a toss for popularity.' There was a pause, then she ended, 'Don't get too close, Liz. I'd hate you to get hurt.'

'I don't want her to get hurt,' said David Oldfield sadly.

'Robert's father is innocent.' Pat spoke the words with what she thought was conviction. 'From what Sal says . . .'

'I'm old-fashioned.' He stroked her hair. 'Old-fashioned enough to believe in British justice. Robert's biased. So is Sal.'

'So,' she said gently, 'is everybody who loves somebody. You, me, Sal, Robert . . . everybody. It's part of it.'

'Meaning I'm biased?'

'I'd think less of you if you weren't.'

'I try not to be,' he sighed. 'Biased one way, biased the other. I want her to be happy, but I don't want her to be hurt. I wish I knew *which* way to be biased.'

'Over-protection,' she murmured and it was a gentle warning.

'I know. I'm an old hen.'

'You're an old hen,' she agreed. 'That's part of it, too. One of the nice parts.' She tilted her head and looked up at him. 'Darling, give her a chance. A chance to be hurt if things go that way. If we're still here for her to run to – if we never say "I told you so" – that's the important thing.'

'Wisdom,' he said softly. He touched her forehead with his lips. 'Not logic, wisdom. Why men love women. Why I love you.'

She allowed a coquettish smile to touch her lips and said, 'Not the *only* reason I hope.'

And almost thirty miles away a man lay awake and stared into the darkness and through a cell window and almost choked on pity for himself. A pitiful man with a lifetime of shabby secrets behind him and a lifetime of enclosed nothingness ahead of him. He stared at a single star visible through the tiny pane, and such was his self-centredness that he was blind to the star as, over the years, he'd been blind to all things beyond his immediate reach. A grown man with the emotions and petulance of a child; unaware of his own faults and hurt that the world had found fault in him.

The silliest woman can manage a clever man; but it needs a very clever woman to manage a fool.

Plain Tales from the Hills
Rudyard Kipling

Saturday was an empty day, filled to the brim with trivialities. The weather had changed; a cold, bright sun shone from beyond opaque cloud cover and, out of the chilling breeze, it might have been a day in May hinting at a long, hot summer. Gardeners hurried out to complete the last of their winter digging. Motorists counted the notes in their wallets, then drove out to beauty spots for a final taste of freedom before the shackles of winter clamped them indoors. The ramblers and the walkers took to the Tops, laden like pack-mules with the lumber of their recreation. The football terraces filled and shirted young men, puffed with their own importance, were roared on to perform prima donna stupidities around a game which was no longer a game.

And Carol Drever came home.

Liz drove her in from the hospital. Snout was waiting, but Snout was balked; Babs timed it perfectly and telephoned the local police station. 'I'm a friend of Detective Chief Inspector Hoyle. There's a man – a fat, suspicious-looking character – hanging around outside the house. He's definitely up to no good. I have a feeling he's contemplating a break-in. Could you send an officer round, please? I'm quite sure he needs questioning, if only from the point of view of crime prevention.' Therefore, while Carol was bustled into the house, an indignant Snout fumed and antagonised two motor patrol officers who, because of his ill-manners, deliberately kept him occupied and refused to believe proof of his honesty and profession without unnecessary verification.

Robert and Babs were waiting. Anne was behind the counter of a travel agency. There was much dabbing of eyes, elbow-holding, unsteady progress across the carpet, patting of cushions and positioning of footrests. Quite a to-do, in fact, and Carol accepted it as her due and, in a slightly vapourish way, enjoyed it. 'Are you sure you're comfortable, mother?' 'Yes Robert, dear, I *think* so.' 'A hot drink? Coffee?' 'Would you, Liz darling? I don't know what we'd do without you.' That sort of thing by the pailful, but not from Babs.

Babs said, 'Welcome home,' and left it at that. The other stuff she watched with a slightly sardonic smile. It was the first time she'd seen this sister-in-law of hers since William's arrest, and she seemed to be trying to penetrate the surface seeking, without much success, something deep inside.

Liz disappeared into the kitchen. Robert was in the bedroom, hunting for slippers.

Babs said, 'How's William?'

'What?' Carol stared. 'How do I . . .'

'Oh, yeah.' The mock-apology and the mock-remembrance had the silent, blistering quality of paint-remover. 'I forgot. You've been too busy feeling sorry for yourself for less important things.'

'You've no right to . . .'

'Get the sheets changed, honey. I've been using your bed.'

Robert hurried in with the slippers.

'Thank you, Robert. You're a darling.'

'A real darling,' echoed Babs softly.

The detective constable said, 'But he's already been convicted, sir.'

'Ever heard of Dreyfus?' said Hoyle heavily.

'Yes, sir.'

He was a young D.C. Bright and ambitious. Not too popular, not too unpopular; having a natural flair for keeping the world at arm's-length, but close enough to study the interplay of likes and dislikes, strengths and weaknesses of those he worked with and those he policed. Hoyle liked his style, and in Hoyle's opinion this one was going places given the time and the opportunity.

Hoyle dropped the heavy file on the surface of the desk and said, 'An open mind. *Open* . . . not empty. Forget cover-ups. That's not what I'm looking for. It isn't the strongest case in the world. It never was. Much of it bricks without straw, but honest bricks and we hadn't much straw. I want a new mind looking for mistakes. Genuine mistakes. For or against. There might not *be* any. *I* can't find any. Maybe I'm too close. Been in this job too long. It was a very emotive case. Too damned emotive.'

As he reached for the file, the D.C. said, 'And if I find anything?'

'Let me know. Who the hell it is – even if it's *me* – let me know.'

'Yes, sir.'

Hoyle read the thought in the expression of the D.C. and said, 'I know it's too late, constable. There's little, if anything, we can do. But at least we should *know*.'

'If there *is* anything,' said the D.C. woodenly.

Hoyle nodded, and said, 'Take your time. There's no deadline. An exercise, if you like. Give you some idea of how a murder file's built up.'

'Yes, sir. Thank you, sir.'

'That's all,' said Hoyle wearily. 'Just keep it safe. Locked away in your locker, somewhere. Don't take it home. Safer that way. And don't let too many other people thumb through it. I'm picking *your* brains ... not organising a referendum.'

Colin Yardley used Saturdays to check the storeroom stock and the yard stock. To keep the books recording his VAT up to date. To check the bills and, as far as possible, organise the coming week's work. As always, he wondered whether he could carry *two* apprentices. As always, he doubted it. Two men, himself and the one apprentice because these days lads didn't work for buttons in return for being taught a trade. These days a lad – even one straight from school who knew damn-all and was only fit for carrying the tools – had to be paid a wage. A good wage. A bigger wage than *he'd* handled even after he'd qualified. My God! Talk about 'small businesses'. Every week one or more went down the river. This one, for example. Once upon a time a little gold mine. Today? Christ, he had to tread water just to keep afloat. And that bloody wife of his ...

She entered the office at that moment. She wrinkled her nose as the background smell of putty and tallow offended her stuck-up nostrils. He noticed it, but ignored it. To him the smell was one of work. Of success ... albeit a very limited success. When they couldn't afford putty, when they couldn't afford tallow, they'd *really* be up the creek.

She said, 'I've been thinking.'

He resisted the temptation to ask, 'What with?' and instead made a soft grunting sound.

'Those two people you were talking to last night. Wasn't one of them the detective in charge of the Drever enquiry?'

'Yes.'

'What did they want?'

'Clearing up a few details,' he said vaguely.

'What sort of details?'

'Bits and pieces. Loose ends.'

'But he's been sent to prison.' She looked puzzled. 'How can there be bits and pieces?'

'Loose ends.' he repeated.

'All right,' she insisted, 'how can there be loose ends?'

'I dunno.' He moved his shoulders in a dismissive movement.

'They were with you long enough.'

'Leave it,' he grunted.

'Is there something I don't know?' she accused.

'Course not,' he lied.

'Because if there is ...'

'Can't you see I'm busy?' he snapped. 'Can't you see I'm up to the neck in it?'

'It's important.'

'*This* is important. A bloody sight more important than last night.'

'I think you're hiding something,' she said coldly.

'What the hell have I to hide?'

'I don't know. That's what I'm ...'

'Look!' Like many small men he had a fiery temper. He glared his anger and snarled, 'Get on with *your* work, and leave me to get on with *mine*.'

Having settled his mother, Robert retired his room to catch up with the reading for the project in hand. He was of an age, a generation, much interested in ecology. Energy and the conservation of energy was his business; the business of any architect of the future. Solar energy. Energy from the wind and the waves. That and insulation. The Scandinavians had the right idea. Somewhere – in one of the college magazines – he'd read an article which, while seeming at first sight to be far-fetched, just *might* be possible. Certainly the author of the article thought so. Even claimed to have made it work in a minor way. Complete insulation; triple-glazed windows, double-cavitied walls, a complete, draught-proof isolation from outside temperature. And the body-warmth of the people in room kept the inside temperature steady and comfortable. No fires, no heating: just *people*. Would it work? And if it *would* work, what about the expense? A gimmick perhaps? Or something new and revolutionary, waiting for the kinks to be ironed out before it could be used on a larger scale?

Robert Drever – architect would be a man passionately interested in beauty of line and perfection of proportion, but of equal importance would be the functional side of things. To live in comfort need not equate with wealth or ugliness. Simple dignity *could* dovetail in with warmth, and at the same time the preservation of what fossilised fuels the world still had to offer. All it needed was thought. A mind ready to accept possibilities. Concentrated study of the various problems which at first sight seemed incompatible.

There was a knock on the door. He raised his head from his book and called for whoever was outside to enter.

Liz came into the room and said, 'If you're busy . . .'

'No. It can wait.'

'Your mother.' She sat on the edge of the divan bed. 'We're going to tell her today. Babs suggested it. I agree.'

'Oh.' He closed the book, carefully placing a postcard in position as a book-mark.

'She has to know,' explained Liz. 'The Linley woman was quite adamant. She intends confronting her.'

'I can't think why. I can't think what good it will do.'

'Nor I,' admitted Liz. She hesitated, gave a quick smile of reassurance, then added, 'She – er – she's very civilised. I don't think she'll cause trouble. I'm sure she won't.'

'No.' It was neither agreement nor disagreement. Just something to say. He lowered his gaze, looked at his fingers and in a low voice said, 'It's odd . . . feels odd.'

'What's that?'

'The woman. The last victim.'

'Yes?'

'If this Mrs Linley is right. She's our half-sister.'

'Robert, you mustn't . . .'

'Isn't she?' He looked up, and his face was clouded by doubt and worry. 'If she's right, she *has* to be.'

'Yes.' Liz nodded. 'I suppose she is.'

'Liz, I . . .' He moved his hands in a tiny, helpless gesture. 'I don't *feel* anything. Since I realised. It's made no difference.'

'Why should it? She's still a stranger.'

'But closer to us than – y'know – than *you* are.'

'Blood ties,' said Liz gently.

'Yeah, I suppose.' But he wasn't satisfied.

Liz tried to understand. In part *did* understand, but not fully. The age gap precluded complete understanding. Robert's standards were modern-day standards; based on non-conformity, yet more hidebound than those of the Edwardian era; hard-headed yet in their own way more romantic than all the wild romanticism of the Bronte sisters. Different. A new and shining base-line beyond the comprehension of a generation other than that which had drawn that base-line. Morality meant nothing. Nor did immorality. The murdered woman had been of his own blood. There had been kinship. His half-sister. And he felt nothing and, because he felt nothing, there was guilt. Logic could not remove it. An older generation could never understand it. It was there and it would remain, because the murdered woman would always be a stranger.

'I hope mother doesn't treat her too badly,' he muttered.

'Who?' Liz still wasn't on the same wavelength.

'Mrs Linley. Mother can be hurtful sometimes.'

Liz smiled and said, 'I don't think you need worry.'

'Is she . . . nice?' It was an awkward, hesitant question.

'Mrs Linley?'

'Y'know – is she . . .'

'She can take care of herself,' Liz assured him. 'It won't be a slanging match. I'm sure of that.'

Bill Drever said, 'Christmas.'

The one word. To anybody else it would have been meaningless. Even to Mary Drever it meant little on its own. But it was Bill's way. To him it was a form of verbal chapter heading. An indication that the subject-matter he was about to discuss concerned the forthcoming holiday period.

Mary said, 'It'll soon be here.'

And this, too, was meaningless out of the context of their own form of communication. Merely her way of letting her husband know that they were about to talk about Christmas.

Bill made a gentle smacking sound with his lips, then mused, 'I think we'll do summat different this year.'

'Different?'

There was surprise almost amounting to shock in the question. To Bill Christmas had always been *Christmas*. The one holiday of the year when *nothing* changed. Carols on the radio or television, but only after Bonfire Night, and never after Twelfth Night. But between those two dates, carols. A great gorging of carols; as if to fill the whole system with enough carols to last the rest of the year. And *Messiah*. The Friday before the twenty-fifth; Lessford Choral Society. That, too, was a 'must'. Plus, of course, any broadcast or television presentation of *Messiah*. *Messiah* to Bill was almost as important as the carols. No other oratorio mattered a damn. But *Messiah*, well it was *MESSIAH* . And the midnight service, Christmas Eve. The only time he saw the inside of the parish church, but the one service he never missed. And after the service their toast to each other in best whisky; and the kiss which said 'Thank you' for one more year of contented marriage. Then Christmas Day; Christmas dinner – midday dinner Yorkshire style, not early evening dinner like the Southerners – with a turkey and trimmings, and Christmas pudding ablaze with brandy sauce, and mince pies. And, at least in the past, with William and his wife and their two grandchildren. And the presents. And the cigars. And the fruit and the nuts, and the ...

Had she been asked, she could have written a list, giving times and activities, people and anecdotes. An annual blueprint, which never varied. And now, 'I think we'll do summat different this year.'

A shy smile, tinged with sadness, touched Bill's lips.

'It's not a holiday for you, Mother. It's never been a holiday for you.'

'I'm not grumbling. I've never grumbled.'

'No,' he agreed. 'But you can't deny it. No holiday for you. Baking and cooking and that. And nobody comes round to give you a hand.'

'I don't need anybody.'

'Any road ...' He paused, as if to give himself a second's

readiness before speaking words of great portent. 'This year we're going away. This year we'll lock up and let somebody else do all the work.'

'Where?' And the question was touched with mild panic.

'A cruise.'

'A *what*.'

'They're advertised.' Having started, his enthusiasm gathered momentum. 'Two weeks, thereabout. Christmas cruises. Not far. Just calling in at a few places. Foreign ports. That sort of thing. And getting your feet up. Letting other people do all the graft.'

'Nay, lad. I've never been out of the . . .'

'We can afford it.' His chin jutted slightly. 'Damn it, we *deserve* it. We've taken a bloody hammering these last few weeks. I reckon we can . . .'

'No.' She shook her head with absolute finality. 'No, Bill. I don't like running away.'

'Who said owt about . . .'

'And if we get on a ship, what then? They'll know. Strangers. Happen people we don't even like. They'll know who we are.'

'Not if we don't . . .'

'They'll find out.' Resigned sadness was in her tone. 'Nowt surer. They'll find out. Somebody will. Then we'll be like a peep-show. We'll wish we hadn't. We'll wish we'd stayed at home.'

He scowled. Extra lines folded into his forehead and the corners of his mouth turned down. It had seemed such a good idea. A *real* Christmas present for both of them. But, dammit, she was right. Some nosey bugger *would* ferret it out and then what? Not much point in spending brass on a cruise, if you had to hide away in your cabin all the time. A poor Christmas. A *bloody* poor Christmas.

He muttered, 'Happen you're right, Mother. Y'know, happen you're right.'

'It was a nice thought,' she comforted him. 'A very nice thought, lad. Don't think I don't appreciate it.'

In later years when they talked of it there was a diversity of opinion. And yet had you asked any of them – Liz, Babs or

Robert – they might have admitted that they didn't know what to expect. Tantrums, perhaps? Carol throwing one of her song and dance acts? Or perhaps numbness? The inability to fully comprehend?

What they *didn't* expect was the calm acceptance which was so out of character.

Nor was there any way of easing into it. Liz had tried. 'Carol, we think William was wrongly convicted.'

That had produced raised eyebrows. Something not much in excess of bored, non-interest.

'We don't think he killed the last girl and, if he didn't kill *her*, he didn't kill any of them.' Because this softly-softly approach wasn't getting anywhere, Babs had jumped in with both feet. 'He wouldn't kill his own daughter, and we've reason to believe that's who she was. His own daughter.'

'Don't be ridiculous.'

Robert urged, 'Mother, accept it. Accept the possibility. If the Linley girl *was* Dad's daughter, he wouldn't kill her.'

'Robert dear, I'm sure you've got work to do. I think you should go do it.'

'But Mother . . .'

'Please Robert.'

'Mother, you *have* to . . .'

'Robert, I think you should,' murmured Liz.

It was touch and go. Both Liz and Babs could see that open rebellion simmered beneath the surface. What they didn't realise was the true reason for that rebellion; that, by the yardstick of the youngster, he was being ordered to deny the existence of his own kin; that this, plus the guilt he felt at the absence of feeling, was threading his particularly 'modern' conscience through a mental shredding machine. It was therefore touch and go, and when he at last mumbled, 'If – if you say so,' and walked from the room, he felt like a traitor.

Liz and Babs continued the attempt to make Carol understand.

'He's innocent. He *said* he was innocent.'

'He was found guilty.'

'What the hell does that mean? Twelve jerks in a jury box.'

'Babs, I know you mean well, but he was *found* guilty. It's

155

something I'm prepared to live with.'

'Even if he's innocent?'

'He's *not* innocent. I keep telling you he was . . .'

'Hold it right there!' Babs planted her feet apart, and glared down at this impossible sister-in-law of hers. The tone matched the blazing eyes, and the time for genteel persuasion was past. She snapped, 'Get it into that ivory skull of yours. He's in jug and maybe he *shouldn't* be there. Just maybe, but 'maybe' is enough for me. If he *should*, okay he can rot there for the rest of his life for all I care. But if not . . .' The nostrils quivered with a fury she did nothing to conceal. 'He's my brother, honey. Never forget that. He's my brother, and I shall do something a damn sight more constructive than putting a razor blade to my wrist. Let me tell you something, my lady. You don't give a toss about the murders. That's not what's getting up your nostrils. Not the murders. Not the abominations. What you can't stomach is the thought that brother William has been dipping his wick in other lamps than yours. For *that* he deserves punishing. For *that* he can stop in jail as far as you're concerned. If topping was still in vogue for *that*, you'd stand by and see him topped.'

It got through. Such was the power and the passion, it couldn't *not* get through.

Carol curled her lips and said, 'Some of us have moral principles.'

'Yeah. And "some of us" are stupid bitches, but haven't the sense to realise it.'

Bryant tried to analyse his feelings. A man, honest to the point of brutality, he knew that while on the face of things he was something of a catch for a middle-aged spinster, he was in fact a man well set in his ways. Liz was a pleasant companion, but for the moment that's *all* she was. Probably even a sister-substitute.

The two of them – Bryant and his sister May – had been inseparable. After the death of their parents they'd set up home together. He with his ever-expanding record collection. She with her passion for poetry and a slim volume of romantic verse to her credit. A strange and unusual relationship. People had talked, but who the devil cared about people talking? Theirs had been an incestuous love without the complication of carnality. Recognised as such. She'd never looked at another man, nor he at another woman. They'd wished to die together. That had been the measure of the bond.

And now Liz.

For four years he'd mourned May. Holding himself tight, refusing the temptation of the drugs at his disposal, loving the memory of her as much, almost more than, he'd loved her frail beauty when she'd been alive. Reading her poems had choked him. His own great passion for music had torn the wound open, again and again.

And now Liz.

Did he unconsciously see in Liz somebody who might replace May? If so, it was unfair. Unfair to May. Unfair on Liz. Because Liz was so unlike May in so many ways. The simple, uncomplicated honesty was there, of course; in that they *were* alike. But Liz lacked May's childlike naivety. Liz, although kind, could see fault, whereas May had been blind to all fault ... and he might not take too kindly to fault-finding even where justified. On the other hand he was too old (and, come to that, Liz was too old) for any serious thoughts concerning a Pygmalion re-shape.

Things weren't simple. Nothing was simple. As a medic he knew that. 'Complications have set in.' A neat little rounded phrase. A very handy, use-at-any-time phrase. Polite, too. Much nicer than saying, 'There's a cock-up, and we haven't sorted it out yet.'

Well, 'complications had set in' as far as his own life was concerned, and to un-cock the cock-up might take some time.

Babs telephoned *The Wounded Hart* and spoke to Ruth Linley. It was a very businesslike call. No frills. No unnecessary please-and-thank-you talk. Without having met, each recognised in the other a woman not given to wasting time on too much courtesy.

'Babs Drever. That's the name I use.'

'Do I know you?'

'You know damn well you don't, but don't let that throw you. You want to see my sister-in-law, Carol Drever.'

'I intend seeing her before I leave Beechwood Brook.'

'Six o'clock tomorrow evening.'

'I think I might be able to ...'

'That's when. Take it or leave it.'

'I'll arrange dinner. Will Liz and her doctor friend ...'

'Not at *The Wounded Hart*. At Carol's home.'

'Oh?'

'The medic won't be there. Just Carol, Liz and me.'

'You sound sure I'll come.'

'Lady, I don't give a damn. Nor does Carol, nor does Liz. *You* held out the begging bowl. If you want it filling, that's where and when.'

'*You'll* be there?'

'Count on it.'

A soft laugh came over the wire and Ruth Linley said, 'I'm rather looking forward to meeting *you*, dear.'

Having replaced the receiver, Ruth Linley dialled a number.

Less than thirty minutes later, Snout was removed from his post. There was much cursing and swearing, but the editor of *The Bordfield and Lessford Star* was in no mood for compromise. Saturday was his day off, and the call he'd had from the newspaper's proprietor hadn't sweetened his temper.

'It's dead,' he snapped.

'The hell it's ...'

'Shift yourself, Snout. Don't waste time arguing.'

'God Almighty! I *tell* you ...'

'Snout, if I never gave an order in my life, I'm giving one now. Move it. Shift yourself. Find the nearest bloody sewer and hide yourself in it. That or you're finished. Not just with *The Star*. I'll make it my business to see you don't even get space in *The Beano*.'

And poor Anne. Her feet ached, her hands were grubby from handling badly printed brochures and there'd been more than the usual run of impossible enquiries. 'Miss, my wife and I are planning a holiday in Spain early next year. Obviously we wish to travel together. But I detest flying and my wife equally detests sailing. What do you suggest?' And oh, that stupid pig of a manager. Coming up close and breathing bad breath into her face while he mouthed his never-ending platitudes. 'Miss Drever, you must sell them *something*. A good salesperson never allows a customer to leave empty-handed. They come in here half-committed. All it needs is gentle persuasion.' God! What a way to earn a pittance.

And now Mother was playing up for all she was worth.

'Anne, dear, they want me to meet that ridiculous Linley woman.'

'I think you should. If Daddy's innocent . . .'

'He isn't, darling. I was there. I saw him when they passed sentence.'

'But Mummy he pleaded Not Guilty. He said he *didn't*.'

'The police don't make mistakes, my dear. Not those sort of mistakes.'

Nevertheless, and perhaps because of the day's niggling little irritations, Anne had stuck out, and Carol had made quite a production number out of her resignation. 'Nobody's on my side. *Nobody*. I wish I'd done it. What I set out to do. I wish you and Liz hadn't stopped me.'

And Anne had snapped, 'Mother, don't be such a goose,' and walked out of the room.

And now even Liz and Babs.

Liz said, 'Anne, pet, you mustn't be here.'

'Why not? I'm . . .'

'Three is enough.'

Babs added, 'Honey, three's the limit. Any more and it might look like intimidation. Just Liz and me and your mother. Robert's going to his girl friend's house. You find somewhere to go.'

'I could stay in my room.'

'Not good enough,' said Babs. 'The temptation might be too strong. I want you out. Away. Somewhere where I know you can't pop in and screw things up.'

Later, while recalling the small argument, Anne wondered a little about the phraseology used by Babs. The use of the pronoun 'I'. As if *she* was the one the Linley woman was coming to see. Not Carol. That or . . .

But the day drew to a close. Each went to bed and each slept – or tried to sleep but couldn't – and Sunday arrived, quietly and without fuss. Nevertheless, a special day. *The* day. A stick-or-bust day, and to that extent a day to be feared perhaps. And yet none knew *why* it should be a fearful day; what there was about it, what might happen, to make it one of the special days of their whole lives. Just that it was. Just that it had that 'feel'.

... a wife who likes being a
woman, which means she likes
men, not elderly babies.

Travels With Charley
John Steinbeck

The bulk of Sunday was spent setting the stage. That in effect was what it boiled down to. The Hoovering, the polishing, the checking of the cigarette box and booze cabinet, the re-filling of the lighter and the bringing-in of an extra armchair. Thereafter the strategic positioning of occasional tables, the making of sandwiches and the grinding of coffee beans. Liz and Babs worked hard at it while Carol watched with open contempt.

'Just who are you expecting? The Queen of Sheba?'

'Honey, if she can help that dumb brother of mine, I'll hire Buck House for the day.'

The weather was clear and dry, therefore the windows were opened to allow the air in the house to sweeten. Curtains were touched and straightened. Cushions were thumped and fluffed. Rugs were positioned with meticulous care.

Robert, with some hesitation, prepared himself to meet Sal's parents. He looked so quietly unhappy that Liz tried to jolly him up a little.

'They're nice people, pet.'

'I don't know. I've never met them.'

'They're responsible for Sal. The way she talks, the way she acts. They *have* to be nice people.'

'I suppose.' He frowned, then muttered, 'I should be here. I should be hearing what this Linley woman has to say.'

'A verbatim report. Promise.'

'Still, I should . . .'

'No, you shouldn't. You should be doing what you're going to do. Never fear. Aunt Babs and I will look after your mother.'

Anne, too, fought to stay, but Babs wouldn't even consider it.

'Anne, honey, I might want to use some spicey language.'

'I know all the . . .'

'I don't doubt it. But you being here might cramp *my* style.'

'Babs, you won't let her . . .'

'Sweetheart, she won't even *breathe* without my personal go-ahead. Now off you go. What have you planned?'

'There's a coffee-house-cum-disco we thought we might . . .'

'Great. Go dislocate your pelvis. Enjoy yourself.'

Later Liz put her foot down. She'd met Ruth Linley; she knew what to expect. 'Whatever she is, she has class. It may be surface gloss, but we're *not* going to play dustcart to her Lord Mayor's Show.' Babs was all for it; she expected a fight – indeed she *hoped* for a fight, although she wasn't too sure about the *reason* for fighting – and it was with real enthusiasm that she proclaimed her intention of donning what she was pleased to call her 'battle colours'.

Carol (as was to be expected) raised objections.

'Look, I don't know the woman. I've no real desire to even meet her. Why should I primp myself up for a complete stranger?'

'First impressions,' said Babs. 'Start by knocking their eye out ... you're half way home.'

Liz said, 'Carol, she's *going* to see you. She's that sort of a woman. Babs has fixed it to be here – on your home ground – don't ruin that slight advantage by not caring about your appearance.'

Carol capitulated, but without grace, and during the later afternoon there was much bathing and hair combing and decisions concerning dresses. Carol had returned to her own bedroom, Babs had moved into Anne's room and Anne had moved in with Liz. Liz tapped on the bedroom door and entered without waiting.

'Can you just ...'

She stopped. She hoped she hadn't seen what she *thought* she'd seen as Babs hurriedly closed the shoulder-sling handbag with undue haste.

'Uhu?' Babs turned and the smile was just a little forced.

'Was that ...'

'What can I do for you, honey?' The interruption was a deliberate indication that Liz should not ask questions. Gentle and with a smile. But firm and very positive.

'Er – this ...' Liz held out the neat, but imitation, string of pearls. 'I can't get the catch fastened.'

'Here ... give it.' Babs took the necklace, waited until Liz had turned then with little difficulty snapped the fastener. She said, 'A knack, that's all.'

Liz turned back until she could see the closed handbag.

She breathed, 'For God's sake, Babs ...'

'Check on Carol, eh? And cool it, honey. You worry too much. You even worry about things that aren't your concern.'

She arrived punctually. Almost to the second. The doorbell rang, Liz answered it, and again found herself appraising Ruth Linley as a woman who had once been a real beauty. Who was even today a woman capable of turning heads. Her dress was another two-piece costume. This time deep green, with a blouse of a slightly lighter shade of green and a double string of pearls which were definitely *not* imitation.

She led her into the main room and made the introductions. It was all very polite. Very civilised. The shaking of hands, the motioning to the empty armchair, the offering and acceptance of a cigarette, the offering and acceptance of a drink.

As Liz settled into her own chair, Babs murmured, 'A real hen party.'

Ruth raised her glass slightly, tasted and said, 'Very nice.' Then, to Carol, 'Thank you for your hospitality.'

Carol gave a single, non-committal nod.

'I feel I've known you for a long time. May I call you Carol? My name is Ruth.'

'I haven't even known *about* you until yesterday. I'd prefer Mrs Drever, if you don't mind.'

Babs said, 'Okay, Ruth. You're topping the bill on this show. How do we start?'

'As impetuous as you were on the telephone,' smiled Ruth. 'I rather like that. It saves time.'

'Great. Save móre time.'

'Liz.' Ruth turned her head. 'Before we start, a small favour. Telephone *The Wounded Hart*, and ask to speak to *me*. Be insistent. Even the manager, if you feel so disposed.'

'But that's ridiculous. You're . . .'

'Please.'

'Let the lady have her ounce of glory,' said Babs gently.

Puzzled Liz left her chair and walked to the telephone. Ruth relaxed in her armchair and smoked her cigarette. Babs and Carol listened to one half of a telephone conversation. Babs with a faint smile touching her lips. Carol making great play at indifference.

Liz returned the receiver to its rest and returned to her chair before she spoke.

In a slightly tight tone, she said, 'You're not to be disturbed.

You're in your room having a private dinner party with Alderman and Mrs Marchbanks. The – er ... The manager visited your room, about half an hour ago, and you gave him strict instructions. You were not to be disturbed. Even by a telephone call.'

Babs chucked quietly.

'But *why*?' asked Liz.

'Bugs,' said Babs. 'The lady does not want this conversation taped. It's not *being* taped. But she doesn't know that. If it *was* and certain – er – incriminating words were said . . . she's not even here. Three against three. And one of her three is an alderman, backed up by the manager of a class hotel.' She smiled at Ruth and ended, 'In a nutshell?'

'In a nutshell,' agreed Ruth calmly.

'Which,' added Babs, 'means she feels vulnerable.'

'No, my dear, it means I feel *safe*.'

In a tight, brittle voice Carol said, 'This – this meeting. It's ridiculous. I don't know why on earth . . .'

'She has her reasons,' interrupted Babs.

'Indeed.' Ruth nodded.

Having recovered from the shock of the telephone call Liz said, 'All right. We've all been polite. We've been shocked . . . a little. Let's all stop behaving like children and get on with it. Whatever "it" is.' To Ruth, 'You're here. Please tell us *why* you're here.'

Jazz. Like all music, the great leveller. The meal, while not being a complete flop, had been tense; polite small-talk, with a little too much starch to allow for comfort; an awareness of eyes rather than ears. Not a disaster then but no roaring success. And now Pat and Sal were in the kitchen washing-up and David Oldfield had taken Robert into what he called his Music Room, and for the first time they found common ground and could relax even to even disagree about unimportant things.

The room was a single-storey extension to the house. A purpose-built 'den' whose furnishing, other than two old but comfortable armchairs, was geared to music; the recording, playing and reproduction thereof. A Steinway baby grand claimed pride of place in the centre of the room, but the walls were layered with deep shelves containing the necessities of Oldfield's passion. Tapes, cassettes, record-players, microphones and loud-speakers. Hi-fi, stereo, mono ... even quadraphonic if called for. It was a jazz buff's dream world.

From twin speakers Jack Teagarden swung softly into the last four bars of improvisation around *The Sheik of Araby*. Oldfield fingered a single-note melody line on the piano in order to demonstrate the precision with which the master wove a pattern around the tune, then he leaned sideways, flicked a toggle as the chorus ended and Harry James fronted his own orchestra and exploded from the speakers, jamming away like crazy on the same tune, but at a tempo half as fast again as the Teagarden version.

Oldfield left the piano and, with a grin of pure delight on his face, sank into the empty armchair.

'You have to be stone deaf not to follow this one,' he remarked.

Robert returned the grin and said, 'I prefer the Teagarden version.'

'They're both good.' Oldfield cocked his head on one side. 'Listen for the coda. This was one of his 'on' days. A lip like tempered steel. Nobody else would have *attempted* this sort of playing.'

'Armstrong?' suggested Robert tentatively.

'The daddy.' Oldfield nodded slow, half-agreement. 'Armstrong was a small combo player. All his greats ... never more than half a dozen other musicians. James was big-band. Always. The Goodman orchestra. James led the brass section on every collector's item. He started playing in a circus band. All noise. *Thunder And Lightning Polka*, three times a day at full blast. That sort of thing. That's how he strengthened his lip. That's where his tone comes from. When he leads, nobody's in any doubt.' He paused then almost reluctantly he continued, 'Kenny Baker. Home grown. Played with Ted Heath. *He* can come up to James at his best even today, and he's at an age when most trumpet players have blown themselves out. It makes you think. Just because he's British. He's a session man. Watch the really *big* spectaculars on television. Keep your eye out for the orchestra. Not the man in front. The players. Every time. Baker's leading the trumpets. Lusher's leading the trombones. Session men. Among the best in the world, but because they're British ...'

The Harry James Orchestra ripped into the final chorus, and a man besotted by his own brand of music chatted away as only an enthusiast can, and one by one the barriers fell, the generation gap lessened and music did what talk had been unable to do.

She lighted a fresh cigarette and she talked while the others listened. There was no animation and little emotion in her words; a simple, unhurried tale of a girl who quite cold-bloodedly reached a decision. 'A drunken father who, just for the hell of it, uses his belt on his schoolgirl daughter tends to bring about a jaundiced view of men generally.' And yet she did not seek sympathy. She merely gave facts as they had happened. The fact that her mother had died before her tenth birthday. The fact that she'd been hungry more often than she'd had a filled belly. The fact that a slum was a slum was a slum ... and the oft-quoted 'neighbourliness' of fellow-slum-dwellers belonged to the same stable of fiction as 'honour among thieves'.

'Sixteen was the age,' she said with a smile. She drew on the cigarette. 'I knew the street women. I'd talked with them. I knew the law. That after the girl was sixteen the man was in the clear. That prostitution, *per se*, wasn't against the law. Only the act of soliciting was unlawful.'

Intelligence or animal cunning? Liz listened, but couldn't decide which. A girl who leaves school at the age of fourteen and thereafter works at dead-end jobs for two years. Saves as much as she is able to save. Talks with whores and learns the secrets and the law surrounding her already chosen profession. Quite openly, quite cold-bloodedly, approaches a G.P. and arranges for a monthly check for disease. Hunts around for a two-roomed flat – kitchen and living-cum-bedroom – then buys good second-hand furniture in order to equip it as a 'working place'. Intelligence or animal cunning? Whichever, it was a world and a way of life both disgusting and fascinating.

'I even registered myself as self-employed.' The ready smile expanded into a quiet chuckle of remembrance. 'National Insurance, Income Tax Returns. Everything above-board.'

'Books?' Babs asked the one-word question.

'Of course.'

'For putting the bite on ... if necessary?'

For a moment the eyes flashed anger, then the heat died and in a deceptively calm voice she said, 'Babs, you are still not getting the picture. Nothing illegal. Nothing! I set myself a target and when I reached that target I was going to retire. No "previous convictions". Nothing sordid. Nothing . . .'

'Nothing *sordid*!' Carol's murmured exclamation held absolute contempt.

'Carol, my dear.' She paused long enough to draw on the cigarette. 'A married man screws around with another man's wife. *That's* sordid. Both him and her. The other thing? Check through the ermine and coronets. Go far enough back. I'm no socialist, but if it was good enough for them, it was good enough for me.'

'We will,' said Pat with mock severity, 'show a little more respect for the family china.'

Sal smiled a watery smile and tried not to fumble quite as much as she stacked crockery into the kitchen wall-cabinet. From the Music Room the sound of the Basie Orchestra reached the kitchen without any effort. *Jumpin' at the Woodside* had never been intended as a zephyr-like sound. Played by any outfit, its aim was to shake the cobwebs from the rafters. Played by the Count Basie Orchestra of the late '30s, complete with the legendary 'Basie blast,' it seemed to make the walls of the house vibrate.

'He'll deafen him,' wailed Sal.

'He might even *like* it.'

'Who on earth likes . . .'

'The man of the house does, darling. And it's *his* house.'

'I think,' Sal swallowed. 'I think he's testing him in some way.

'It's possible,' agreed Pat with a smile.

'In that case, it's not fair.'

'Sweetheart,' Pat became suddenly very serious. 'Sweetheart, if Robert's your man, he'll sit there with a grin on his face and take it. Whether he likes it or not.'

There was a near-hypnotic quality in the manner in which Ruth told her story. The tone was almost soothing despite the subject-matter. Like a bishop using bargee language from the pulpit. Liz, Babs, even Carol *had* to listen. More than that, they were made to understand.

That first flat. 'Word gets round. That's the first thing I

discovered. Word of mouth. Men who regularly use a *fille de joie* – not the casual one-night-standers, but the men, single and married, who eventually make up a regular clientele – form a loose-knit free-mansonery. They want the best at a reasonable price. Not give-away. No enthusiastic amateurs. A reasonable price, cleanliness and a knowledge of each punter's taste. Like a good restaurant serving good food and no rip-off when the bill arrives.' And to Ruth that's what it was. That was what it had been from the start. A service. Paid for, delivered and enjoyed . . . with no strings attached.

Before she was twenty, she could afford her own flat. A place near the centre of Lessford above a parade of shops. Living room, kitchen, bathroom and two bedrooms. One to work in, one to sleep in. Decorated and furnished, with no real concern for expense.

There was a pause while Liz re-filled the glasses. Ruth took a cigarette case from her handbag, flipped it open and held it in turn to Liz, then Babs, then Carol. Liz and Babs took the offered cigarette without hesitation. Carol gave the impression of being about to refuse, then changed her mind and she, too, took one. Before Ruth could produce a lighter, Liz took the lighter from the shelf and held it in turn to each cigarette. That was how strange the atmosphere in the room had become. 'Mutual civilised contempt'. The phrase snagged on Liz's mind. It summed up everything. A whore arguing not merely the necessity, but also the respectability, of whoredom. And, moreover, doing it well. Almost convincing her audience. Almost!

Babs sipped her re-filled glass and murmured, 'It obviously pays.'

'There are certain built-in dangers.' Ruth took the remark at its face value. She deliberately ignored the possibility of sarcasm.

The 'built-in dangers' were the parasites and the mentally abnormal. The would-be pimps and 'minders'. The kinky types whose only desire was to humiliate. 'Like all professions, it calls for discipline. It calls for self-discipline.' Small-time hoodlums trying to form themselves into various 'firms' saw in this up-and-coming *lorette* a steady source of income. She was propositioned. She was threatened. She always refused. And when things became a little frightening she fought back. 'I caused no trouble.

I was doing nothing illegal and a few of my punters – regular clients – were policemen in high places. *They* were my "protectors" and I paid them through rates and taxes.' Again word got round. Again word of mouth. This one didn't scare, and this one could (and would) bite back.

As for the kinks. The perverts. No whips, no chains, no outrageous geegaws. 'You go to a chemist knowing you can buy branded medicines over the counter. Various medicines for various ailments. You can't buy L.S.D. You can't buy marijuana. To get *those* things you find the nearest sewer. I ran a respectable business. Within the law. I had rules which I kept.'

They sat in the living room and talked. It was no longer strained small-talk. Oldfield seemed genuinely interested, and Robert was relaxed enough to express views without hedging those views with implied apology.

'So,' said Oldfield, 'you're going to be an architect?'

'Hopefully, sir.'

Sal said, 'He'll do it at a trot. Won't you Rob?'

'I don't find it *that* easy,' said Robert with a smile.

Oldfield said, 'Last year we saw the two Liverpool cathedrals. For the first time. I couldn't make up my mind about the R.C. cathedral.'

'The "pepper pot",' grinned Robert.

'Yes, you can understand why the locals call it that.'

'It's modern,' said Robert. 'It's a new design. The other one – the C of E cathedral – that's how people *expect* cathedrals to look. It's magnificent but in effect a carbon copy of every other cathedral.'

'Is that bad?' asked Oldfield.

'No, sir. Not *bad*. But these days we have the tools and the know-how and the material. The others – York Minster for example – that's all they *could* build. They did it magnificently. They stretched themselves to the absolute limit. Today we can do that without too much difficulty. I think we should stretch *our* selves. Try for something different, and hope we achieve something better.'

'There is a limit,' argued Oldfield. 'You reach excellence ... where do you go from there?'

'Look, sir.' The hint of mischief touched Robert's eyes. 'Take jazz. The Original Dixieland Jazz Band. The King Oliver band. They were good. The best of their time. With what they had they created something new. But Ellington – at the Cotton Club – he had something extra and created something better. Then Ellington again – towards the end of his life – something extra. Experiments. Better arrangements. Better made instruments. Something even *better*. The same with architecture. The two Liverpool cathedrals, see? The C of E one. That's like an outfit with better players and better instruments still playing like King Oliver. The R.C. one. That's like Duke Ellington trying for something new. New tools, new techniques, new minds. Trying for something different. With luck ... *better*.' Robert suddenly realised he'd been riding a personal hobby horse. He blushed and said, 'I'm sorry, sir. It's just that ... I'm putting it badly.'

'No, no.' The bond between the youth and the man was sealed. No thought was given to the subject they'd most feared. Oldfield leaned forward a little in his chair and said, 'I can see exactly what you mean.'

'And *I*,' sighed Pat, 'can see two grown men talking hens and chickens to death about jazz and cathedrals. God bless us all! We'll have *South Rampart Street Parade* next.'

'That,' grinned Oldfield, 'is an excellent idea.' He pushed himself from his chair. 'The original Bob Crosby Orchestra recording. It's never been bettered.'

Babs found herself experiencing a psychological tug-of-war. This Ruth Linley woman could argue her case, and although she'd never counted herself as a *professional* cocotte, Babs was honest enough to recognise herself as a creature of pleasure. As opposed to that was her upbringing. What she was – what she'd become – was a direct and deliberate rebellion against the strict rule of Bill and Mary Drever. Bouncing from husband to husband. Having affairs. Being a mite choosey, but at the same time enjoying the thrill of promiscuity. What difference between her pleasure and Ruth's profession? And indeed if there was a difference, who was the more honest?

Certain it was that Ruth had no regrets nor cause for regrets. In what amounted to an almost unique way she'd retained her dignity and her pride. Her honesty was patently obvious. 'A surgeon doesn't practice during his off-duty periods. He doesn't amputate a limb merely because he's bored or to keep his hand in. When he's *on* duty he controls things. He's the expert because he's made it his business to *be* the expert. The difference isn't in degree. The difference is in the chosen disciplines.'

'*Discipline!*' Carol curled her lips. The intent was to show contempt, but it was an empty gesture. Even she had fallen under the spell of this woman who'd imposed herself into their lives.

'Carol, my dear.' The smile was friendly with a hint of pity. 'To discipline a biological urge. Can *you* sleep when you wish to sleep? Not necessarily when you're tired. Urinate only when *you*, not your bladder, decide to urinate? Control every natural desire? It takes practice. A lot of practice. Will-power. Never to lose control . . . of *anything*.'

Liz murmured, 'Yoga.'

'A name,' The gentle smile came and went. 'Mind over matter. The same thing. Surround it with the tinsel of ceremony. It's still the same thing.' And as she continued her story, it was obvious that this near-impossible self-discipline had paid good dividends. By the age of thirty she needed an accountant to deal with her fast growing bank balance. She took advice. She invested. She lived well but not extravagantly. By that time, and having consulted her accountant, she'd decided. By the time she reached her forty-fifth year she'd be a comparatively rich woman. She could retire and enjoy a comfortable degree of luxury for the rest of her life. She planned accordingly. On her forty-fifth birthday – on the day itself – she said goodbye to her last punter, and moved into an already furnished and decorated home on the outskirts of Lessford. In the 'class' district. She could employ a full-time gardener and a respectable living-in woman to see to the heavy chores and the cooking. She'd made it. Not the proverbial hard way, but most certainly the *disciplined* way.

Ruth ended her story. It was the obvious end and, having reached it, she once more handed round her cigarettes and, when they were settled back, smoking and sipping their drinks, she waited.

Carol chewed at her lower lip for a moment, then said, 'You

wanted to see me?'

Ruth nodded politely.

'Not just to tell me the story of your life?'

'No. That was merely required. In order that you might understand.'

'Understand what?' asked Babs.

'William?' Liz added the extra question before Ruth could speak.

'William,' said Ruth gently. Softly.

'You say he's innocent,' said Carol.

'I *know* he's innocent.'

Liz hesitated, then said, 'Your – er – daughter.'

Ruth nodded slowly.

Carol said, 'I don't believe you. What you say – what you've told Liz – I don't believe you.'

'Correction. You don't *want* to believe me.' And like the switching on of a refrigerating unit the atmosphere changed. The intimacy went. The quiet pleasantry disappeared. The unemotional ruthlessness which had taken her to the top showed for the first time. Quietly – flatly – she said, 'What *you* believe. What you *don't* believe. It has no bearing on the truth.'

The Bob Crosby Orchestra thundered out the final bars of the 'cane-break' sequence as Pat entered the room. She flopped into one of the ancient armchairs, blew out her cheeks in mock relief and said, 'Thank goodness *that's* over.'

'I thought . . .'

'Yes, darling, I love it,' she lied, 'but now do me a favour. *Song Of India*. Softly. As they say "with feeling".'

'Of course.'

Oldfield, despite his noisy hobby, despite his stick-in-the-mud profession, was a good and understanding man. He was also methodical. The Tommy Dorsey recording of *Song Of India* was on the turntable within seconds. The volume was turned down and he was in the spare armchair, reaching for Pat's fingers, almost before the old maestro had woven the first few notes of muted magic around the big band version of Rimsky-Korsakov's melody. It was a classic – probably *the* classic – cf big band repertoires. Certainly it topped the not inconsiderable heap of never-to-be-forgotten arrangements recorded by the Dorsey Orchestra and (who knows?) perhaps in some composers' paradise Rimsky-Korsakov himself might have nodded gentle (and strict tempo) approval when it was first waxed.

But it was more than that – far more than that – to Pat and David Oldfield.

Almost dreamily Pat said, 'I'll take the rest just so long as you play this occasionally.'

'It did the trick.' His fingers tightened a little. 'I wouldn't have dared without dear old Tommy encouraging me.'

'You'd have dared,' she smiled. 'I'd have *made* you dare.'

They listened in silence. Held hands, remembered and were happy. Simple, uncomplicated people. Nostalgic and grateful for something around which to wrap their nostalgia.

The record ended and Oldfield relaxed his fingers, but Pat tightened hers.

'Please,' she said softly.

'They'll wonder where ...'

'He's a very nice young man.'

'Of course he is, but ...'

'Give Sal an opportunity. Let her find out *how* nice.'

He tightened his fingers again, chuckled softly, and said, 'You old match-maker, you.'

'D'you mind?'

'No. As you say, he's a very nice young man.'

Babs recalled an incident and realised a truth. Years previously, when she'd been new at the job of general dogsbody, and the idea had been to do a television documentary covering deprivation and graft in Italy. One of those simple-problem-instant-solution slot-fillers; parlour sociology for the masses. The producer, the producer's assistant and Babs had been fortunate; strings had been pulled, palms had been greased and, for all of thirty minutes, they'd talked with the legendary Lucky Luciano. The recognised 'boss of the bosses'; the Mafia big cat who, until he died in 1962, ruled the biggest criminal empire in the world. A quietly spoken man. Neatly dressed, grey-haired and good looking. But with steady eyes, little expression and a decisive turn of phrase. Politely but firmly, Lucky declined to be a party to the proposed documentary, nor did anybody try to dissuade him from his gently expressed decision. Babs had never forgotten that meeting; that elderly man who via his own under-the-counter power had more influence than most statesmen. It was there to see. The gentle but terrifying charisma. The absolute certainty upon which was built a personality quietly confident of out-shining all the tarted-up stars and super-stars in creation. 'The boss of the bosses'. She'd never hoped, never expected, to meet a like character again in her life.

But she had, and the realisation arrived like a side-palm chop at the nape of her neck. Ruth Linley. Her mannerisms, her friendliness, her good-mannered arrogance. *Luciano.* Or as near Luciano as any woman could ever get. Without the empire, without the world wide influence, but most assuredly with that same frightening charisma.

Babs swallowed, then said, 'Honey, we've had the crap. All the rags-to-riches-on-a-casting-couch bullshit. When do we hear something interesting?' And having said it, and in that tone, she was strangely amazed at her own temerity.

For a moment Ruth's eyes narrowed fractionally.

Almost simultaneously (and it was said before the import and impact of Babs's remark had had time to register) Liz said, 'What about love? What about ...' Then she stopped, as Babs's outburst over-rode what she was going to say.

'Love?' Ruth ignored Babs and mused upon the question Liz had been about to ask. She took her time. She opened her cigarette case, chose a cigarette and lighted it. This time she didn't hand the case round to the others. In a soft but deliberate tone she said, 'Yes. I've known love. I've allowed myself to fall in love. Once. With William Drever ...'

'That's a lie!'

'No Carol, dear. It is not a lie. I wish it *was* a lie. But I'm a realist. We loved each other. Despite what *I* was. Despite what *he* was. We loved each other.'

'Don't leave us in suspense,' mocked Babs. 'What *was* he?'

'Your brother. You should know.'

'Your assessment.'

'At the time ...' Ruth drew on her cigarette. 'At the time I thought he was the kindest, most considerate man in the world.

176

But . . .' She moved her shoulders fractionally. 'We always do, don't we?' Nobody answered and she continued, 'Shy. Gauche. Innocent. A year or two younger than myself, but what matter? Age means little – age means nothing – when you're in love.'

'How can anybody be in love with a tart?' croaked Carol.

'It happens, my dear.' A humourless smile touched her lips as she added, 'You should know.' Then before any of them could answer, she continued, 'That's what I thought. You ask for my assessment. That *was* my assessment. I believed it. In those days I was open to such beliefs. I, too, had a certain innocence.'

Babs said, 'A pimp in other words?'

'No!' And for the first time, they saw a flash of real anger. In a distinctly harsher tone she said, 'Lady, you're a dangerous woman. I recognised it when you telephoned. I, too, can be dangerous. Put words in my mouth I haven't said and you'll know *how* dangerous.'

'Not a pimp,' soothed Liz. 'In that case . . . what?'

'The man with whom I was in love.' The composure returned with the ease and suddenness of closing a door. 'In fact a coward. Gutless. A little boy afraid of public opinion. Afraid of what his parents might say. Afraid of what his fiancée might say. Afraid of *everything*. A contemptible little whippersnapper. A nothing!'

'Such a change,' mocked Babs. 'Overnight, too!'

'Almost,' agreed Ruth calmly. 'Even in those days I wasn't a complete day-dreamer. I'd already learned that when the illusionist leaves the stage there's not much point in sitting in an empty theatre. The magic has already gone.' She paused then added, 'Carol, I'm sure, will verify the truth of that.'

'Don't call me "Carol". Dammit, I have a name. For people like you I have a name. It's . . .'

'*It's not "Mrs Drever".*'

Carol blinked, then stared.

Ruth continued, '*I'm* "Mrs Drever". Even while he was engaged to you he married me. To give the child a name. So noble . . . don't you think?' The smile came and went again. '*You're* the one who's been living in sin all these years. *Your* children are the bastards.'

'We – we . . .'

'I don't give a damn what you did. What ceremony you performed. The law still allows a man only one wife . . . and I'm *it*.'

'I – I don't believe you. I . . .'

'Of course you believe me.' The contempt was open and unashamed. 'It's the sort of thing he'd do *and* you know it. It's in character. Completely in character.'

Liz moved from her chair. She placed a protective arm across the trembling shoulders of her sister, and for the first time saw Ruth Linley for what she was.

'Leave,' she said in a low voice. 'You've done what you came to do. Said what you came to say. When I first met you I thought . . .'

'Not yet!' Babs was the one who interrupted. Watching the calm victory on Ruth Linley's face she said, 'Not all of it. Not all of it by a long way . . . am I right?'

Ruth nodded.

'Okay, let's have it. Every miserable crumb.'

'Of course. That's why I'm here.'

Like the last few tatters of bunting after a national celebration, the bits and pieces of what was left of an emotional upheaval blew against the ankles of Bill Drever's mind. They were a nuisance, but they were also a reminder. They worried. They ruined an equilibrium which had been the rock upon which Bill Drever had built his life.

Mary Drever watched from the companion armchair. Her knitting needles clicked quietly, but like most of her kind, her fingers didn't need the assistance of her eyes to fashion wool into garments. She knew her husband and she could read his thoughts. Not involved thoughts. Very simple, very basic thoughts. Knowing him – knowing and living for so long with him and amongst his kind – the reading of his thoughts was no involved exercise.

She murmured, 'Leave it, lad. Let it rest.'

'It won't rest,' he muttered, and the words had a groan-like quality.

'Not if you don't let it.'

And she wondered why men like her husband tortured themselves so. Good men. The salt of the earth. Yeoman stock . . . if such a breed still existed. The work-horse of the human race.

Solid, dependable and neither needing nor demanding fancy frills. But because of this very strength, vulnerable. Unable to understand men who *weren't* like themselves. Unable to appreciate the numberless twists and turns of human personality. Greatness was not for them. Rarely did they collect honours, and when they did they were embarrassed, because they could never understand *why*.

The expression 'God-fearing' touched her mind. Men like Bill *were* God-fearing . . . about the only thing they did fear. No great play was made. Just the so-called Golden Rule. But a man could be God-fearing without being overtly religious. He could be God-fearing without once setting his foot inside a church. Any religion. Any church. She supposed there were men in India, men in Africa, men in China, men all over the world, all like her Bill. All God-fearing, and in some odd way all fearing the same God. Men who tortured themselves with self-guilt whenever they fell short of their own impossible yardstick of perfection.

He lowered his chin onto his chest, rubbed the nape of his neck and mumbled, 'We did all the wrong things, Mother.'

'What?'

He looked up, stared at her with saddened eyes, and in a louder voice repeated, 'We did all the wrong things.'

'Happen.' The needles clicked, the fingers flicked the wool, and in a slightly impatient tone she said, 'All right, we did all the wrong things, but every time for the right reasons.'

It was some story and she told it quietly, but with brazen pride. A story of long-delayed vengeance. A story of that brand of never-ending hatred peculiar to women, and even then only peculiar to a certain type of woman. A child, conceived in passion, then abandoned by one parent and not wanted by the other.

Her logic was at once terrible and impeccable. 'I could have claimed him as my husband. As the father of our child. What good would it have done? It wouldn't have kept him. At the most it would have been a minor financial irritation, and I wanted more than that. Much more than that.'

She brought up the child. She paid for its schooling – she could afford to pay for a private education – then she taught it a trade. A profession. *Her* profession. 'Don't look shocked. I *knew*. The

179

only profession open to a woman worth a damn. The only truly independent profession of our sex. I was living proof of it. I'm *still* living proof of it.' All the tricks, all the guiles, all the rules, all the pitfalls. But not as a partner. As a <u>noviciate.</u> Then she set the daughter up, and left her to make her own name.

Not love. Duty. 'I didn't love her. She stood for my one mistake. The only moment of weakness in my whole life. How could I love her? I lack the so-called mother instinct. I might have had it once, I don't know. I doubt it. But given the opportunity – given William – I might have learned.'

She didn't 'learn' nor even try to. But from a distance she kept an eye on William Drever. On her husband, in fact. As a starter, as a penniless accountant-under-training, little or no vengeance could be contemplated. But come respectability, and come a directorship, things changed. She made herself known, and threatened to shatter the whole fabric of his life.

'The squeeze,' said Babs gently.

'You could call it that.'

'Or I could call it blackmail.'

'I think he owed me something.' Ruth chain-lighted a new cigarette from one only half-smoked. As she squashed the finished cigarette into the ashtray, she said, 'I could have stopped his make-believe marriage. I could have allowed him to go through the motions, then mentioned to the police a little matter of bigamy. I didn't ask for a brass farthing.'

'Until you knew damn well he could cough more than *one* brass farthing.'

Liz said, 'Ten years ago?'

'About that.' Ruth nodded. 'I'm greedy, Liz. It's my nature. I collect all my debts . . . eventually.'

The pattern emerged. The pattern of a weak man, living as husband-and-wife with an impossible-to-please shrew and secretly married to, and under the thumb of, a ruthless and domineering woman. William Drever hadn't a chance. Caught between the red-hot jaws of closing pincers, he did what a weak man always does. He robbed Peter to pay Paul; he cooked the books; he daren't lower the life-style Carol had come to expect and demand, he daren't make a clean breast of his long-past mistake. Respectability was all, he therefore clung to that

180

respectability on a day-to-day basis.

'You're a cow,' said Carol in a low, tight voice.

'Probably,' smiled Ruth. 'But face the facts my dear, I couldn't have been a cow without your active assistance. He was as much afraid of you as he was afraid of me.'

'He's in prison,' said Liz. 'Indirectly you put him there.'

'Indirectly?'

'Surely you can't deny . . .'

'Not *indirectly*. That's the mistake you're making. I put him there. Deliberately. It was no spin-off. He cooked his goose the day he whined about the firm discovering the way he was fixing the books. I wanted money . . . or something in lieu of money.'

It was a monstrous admission to make, and for the moment it silenced the three listeners. They couldn't understand. Not fully. How could they? Carol was merely spoiled and more of a frustrated child than a grown woman. Babs had known roguery and even selfishness beyond the normal, but evil of this magnitude was something new to her. Liz was well out of her depth; only the quiet – almost off-handed – sincerity forced her even to believe.

Babs moistened her lips, then asked, 'And his daughter? Did *she* know about all these fun and games?'

'From what Sal tells us you've reason to believe he's innocent.'

'Yes, sir. We're sure he's innocent.'

The forbidden subject was no longer forbidden. Oldfield and Robert sat in armchairs. Sal and Pat shared the sofa. The two youngsters sipped Coke straight from the cans. Pat held a small glass of sherry and Oldfield was enjoying good whisky. And in one evening – in little more than three or four hours – they were relaxed enough to talk quietly about Robert's father and whether or not he was a monster. Oldfield had brought it up, and Robert hadn't backed away from what he *knew* the older man wanted to discuss.

Very carefully Oldfield said, 'A mistake? You're not suggesting the police grabbed an innocent man rather than have another Yorkshire Ripper on their hands?'

'No, sir.' Robert's voice was steady. 'We think a mistake. Something which wasn't brought out in evidence – something the police didn't know – which should have raised enough doubt to result in an acquittal.'

'For want of proof? Is that what you mean?'

'No, sir. Something he could have proved, but didn't.'

'Why not?'

'Dad!' Sal frowned her annoyance as this ham-fisted father of hers contorted himself and did his best to put his foot in things. 'I don't think you should . . .

'Yes, Sal.' Robert interrupted her. With all the solemnity of his youth he said, 'If I was in his position, *I'd* want to know.'

'Thank you, Robert.' Oldfield nodded his appreciation. 'Now, if you please, tell me why *you* think your father's innocent. I'm not talking about proof. I mean *why*?'

'He's . . .' Robert paused, moistened his lips, then began again. 'The – the crimes don't belong to a man like him. I'm – I'm biased. I realise that. I try not to be – I truly try – but I know I can't possibly be objective about my own father. Nevertheless, I know him. I think I know what he's capable of. I *know* what he's *not* capable of. Those crimes. He – he wouldn't have the guts, sir. I think it takes courage – some sort of courage – to do what was done to those women. He hadn't it. He was – y'know – weak, in some things.'

'You mean he didn't like the sight of blood?'

'No, sir. Not that. Not exactly *that*. But – but women. With mother, for example. He – he couldn't stand up to them. Not like . . .' He paused, then blurted, 'Not like you and Pat.'

'I take that to be meant as a compliment.'

'Yes, sir. Of course. But – but . . .' The lower lip trembled ever so slightly. 'If – if there'd been the closeness. Like you two. The humour. The *happiness*. It's so obvious, but with them . . .'

'Rob!' Sal bounced from the sofa and flung herself at Robert, as if to physically hold back the tears which threatened to spill.

'Your answer, David?' said Pat gently.

Oldfield nodded, then said, 'Subject closed, Robert. Thank you for being so honest.'

'Dad, you've no right to be . . .'

'Sal.' This time Oldfield interrupted. 'He's your friend. I had to know. Now I *do* know. He's your friend, and we'd be honoured if he'd be the friend of the whole family.'

The fundamental fault of the female character is that it has no sense of justice.

Uber die Weiber
Arthur Schopenhauer

Babs had left. She'd expressed her disgust in a typically forth-right manner. 'This whole damn place has turned sour. I need air.' And with that she'd stormed from the house.

Nor was her disgust without foundation. The dam had burst and, as if ridding herself of pus which had been festering inside her, Ruth had launched upon a controlled tirade concerning the child of herself and William. She blamed William, but of course! 'A weak daughter of a weak father.' She herself had guided the young girl along the correct path of professional whoredom. The first rule to be a loner; that above all. To be a loner, to stay within the law and to remain clinically clean. Like a surgeon and an operating theatre. 'I told her. I almost drew diagrams. No in-volvement. A cast-iron reputation for being disease-free. The stupid little bitch *knew*. She didn't just drift into the game. She knew exactly what the responsible punters demanded, but she refused to learn.'

But (weak father, weak child) she'd allowed the porn boys to move in. A consortium of slags, catering for any perversion the kink required, and the result . . .

At which point, Babs had stood up from her chair, hoisted her handbag onto her shoulder, and said, 'I've heard enough, honey. This whole damn place has turned sour. I need air. I'll be back when you've left, and after the house has been fumigated.'

Then she'd walked. Rapidly. Furiously. As if to a known desti-nation, and with little time to spare.

Had she been asked, she would have denied knowledge of that destination, but the knowledge was there. Hers was not the parochial mind of Liz and Carol; hers was a mind honed sharp by an environment in which only the ruthless survived. There was an answer – there was an equation – and because of what she was that answer, the completion of that equation – had deter-mined her destination. *The Wounded Hart*. Into the semi-darkness alongside the hotel, within easy sight of where the cars were parked.

And now she was in the shadows, watching the Merc nose its way into the car park. Squinting at the driver then, as suspicion hardened to certainty, moving from the shadows and arriving at the door of the Merc as Ruth was about to alight.

'A few questions, honey.' Babs blocked Ruth's way. 'Move

over. A few things I'd like to straighten out. Between us two as women of the world.'

'Of course.' Ruth was surprised, but not shocked. The smile was friendly enough, and she obediently shifted her position onto the front passenger's seat. 'You're not quite as innocent as the other two.'

'Bet on it,' murmured Babs, as she climbed into the car, and closed the door. She hoisted the handbag onto her knees then said, 'This girl – this daughter of William – other than the unimportant fact that she was a prozzy . . . a nice girl? Pleasant company? That sort of thing?'

'I thought I made it clear . . .'

'No, honey. Not to me. William you hated. Still hate. The daughter?'

'About as much,' said Ruth bluntly.

'Fine.' Babs nodded slowly, as if one puzzle had been solved. 'And the other two?'

'The other two?'

'Three murders, remember?'

'They were her friends.'

'Part of the anything-for-kicks crowd?'

'That's one way of putting it.'

'And William knew this?'

'I doubt it.'

'But his own daughter. He knew about *her*?'

'Again, I doubt it.'

'He knew her, though? By sight? By name?'

'I keep telling you. I . . .'

'Yeah, honey. You keep telling me. At a guess, you've told me enough.'

It was closing up to ten o'clock. Babs sat on the edge of the bed. She was as near hysterical as a woman of her kind ever can be. She smoked the cigarette in quick, jerky journeys to and from her lips. She was white-faced and there was the hint of a tremble in her frame and the hint of a tremor in her tone.

She watched Liz packing the suitcase and said, 'Everything in, honey. The lot.'

'Babs, I think you should at least stay until . . .'

'All of it, Liz.' The voice was harsh and demanding. 'Then call a taxi. There'll be a train south sometime before morning.'

Liz looked sad, but continued packing.

'Christ!' Babs spoke softly, as if to herself. As if reminding herself of things not yet fully realised. 'Christ, she took some killing. The bitch *wouldn't* die!'

'Look, Babs, if you'd rather not ...'

'Damn it, I *want* to.' The cigarette made another quick journey to and from her mouth. 'That's *why*. Don't you see that? The perfect murder. Who cares if nobody knows? That's what brought her here. To gloat. Knowing – *thinking* – nobody could do a damn thing. Brother William had been made to suck the hammer. All neat and tidy. It was – it was ...'

She almost broke, and Liz had the built-in wisdom to pause in her packing, sit alongside Babs and, in a quiet and calming voice, say, 'Okay, Babs. If it *has* to be told, tell it. Just the once. To me, then to nobody else.'

'Sure.' Babs nodded, then took a deep breath. 'That creep Yardley. Him and his cockeyed yarn about walking the streets during a bridge game. *He* was in her pocket. All he had to do was fanny around on an identification parade. Remember a car number. Jesus Christ, it was so *easy*. Get a bitch like her and some louse who can't keep his fly zipped ... *anything*. Dig *him* out of the woodwork, know what *she* was aiming for. And the cops helped things on their way. They were running scared they might have another Yorkshire Ripper snarl-up on their hands. They were looking at everybody and anybody. But *men*, see? Who the hell expects a *woman* to do these things? Who the hell expects a *mother*?'

She paused for all of thirty seconds. She smoked the cigarette, then she continued, 'William? Okay, he was weak. Weak? I've known stronger gnat's piss. But that was in *her* favour. She'd put the bite on, she'd forced him to cook the books, *that* axe was already on its way. Dammit, he *was* innocent. Innocent enough to figure things as a mistake ... not a frame-up. But *she* knew. She knew she had him by the nuts. And when the jury brought in the verdict, that was his way out. Damnation! He didn't even know the scheming bitch was behind it all. He didn't even *know*. The one thing she couldn't tell him, otherwise he might have fought back. *Might* have, but I doubt it. Brother William wanted to opt out of life. Things had become too complicated. Where he is now, that's where he wants to be. He doesn't even have to *think* for himself.'

Babs leaned forward and rammed what was left of the cigarette into the ash tray on the bedside table. She lighted another, and her hand shook with a neat mix of fury, emotional outrage and disgust.

'I'm – I'm sorry.' Liz found herself asking the question against her own better judgement. 'His own daughter? I mean ...'

'He didn't even *know* it was his daughter.'

'Oh! In that case ...'

'Yeah.' Babs nodded her head vehemently. 'That was the question I asked. That was the question she answered. *If he didn't know his own daughter, Lady Ruth's pretty tale doesn't add up to a toss.*'

'In that case why ...'

'Honey,' sighed Babs heavily, 'old man Kipling knew his onions. All that female-of-the-species stuff. I'll say! She hated her own daughter. For what she was, for who her father was, for everything. You notice? Never once did she use the word "prostitute." Every fancy name she could come up with, but never the *real* name. She hated her daughter, because she'd befouled what *she* figured to be some sort of honourable occupation. She hated her daughter's friends because they were like her daughter. She hated William because he was her daughter's father. Everything! Enough hatred and you're home and dry ... and she had enough and to spare'.

'At a guess, *she* didn't do the killing. Mutilation. She could pay. And there are men willing and able if the price is right.' A sardonic smile touched Babs's lips. 'Don't look shocked, honey. Bastards like that grow fat and shiny in the Smoke. But *she* organised it. Who the hell did it, *she* worked the fix. Put William away.

'She wasn't even satisfied when William went down. She had to sow seed corn for when he came out. Smash William. Smash Carol. Smash Anne. Smash Robert. Smash *everything*. Too many pieces for it ever to be put together again. And, of course, the perfect murder – multiple murder plus abominations – and she had to tell somebody. Carol. Who else. You and me? We were just the standing-room-only audience.

'She – she . . .' Babs choked, then continued, 'She gloated. I swear . . . *gloated*. If she hadn't gloated I don't think . . .' Again she stopped, took a deep draw on the cigarette, then continued, 'The fat slob at the gate. The newshound. She had *him* shifted. No connection, see? Nobody except the family to link her with this address. And we don't count. We're going to *say* that, any-way.'

'Peter,' murmured Liz.

'Who?'

'Peter. Doctor Bryant. He saw her at the hotel.'

'Yeah.' Babs nodded wearily. 'Well, maybe. Maybe she didn't figure him as important. Maybe he *isn't* important. He doesn't know she came to the house. Stack him against Alderman and Mrs Marchbanks. *And* the manager. She even used the alder-man's car. Left her own in its reserved space in the car park. She had everything fixed . . . but good! She was fireproof. If she hadn't – y'know – *gloated*.'

Slowly – almost as if it was being drawn towards it by some unseen force – Babs's free hand pulled the handbag closer. Un-zipped the top, then lifted out the handgun. A Colt Cobra; .32 calibre; two-inch barrel. She stared at it in silence for a moment.

'This – this damn thing,' she croaked. 'For muggers, see? They're around in the Big Place. I – I *needed* it, thought I did.' The tears spilled and ran down her cheeks as she mouthed the words. 'Not for murder. For Christ's sake, not for *that*. I – I . . . The creep who fixed me up with it. I'll – I'll brain the bastard. So help me, I'll brain him. She – she wouldn't *die*. Four shots. God help me, I had to squeeze the bloody trigger *four* times. That's – that's not right. That's not fair.' She raised her face, looked at Liz, pleaded with her eyes, and repeated, 'That's not *fair*. That's like *four* murders.'

'Call it "vermin disposal",' said Liz gently.

'Yeah, vermin disposal'. She dropped the gun back into the handbag, managed a watery smile, and said, 'Y'know, that Ald-erman and Mrs Marchbanks – that manager – they're going to have some very plain and fancy talking ahead of them. In his car, too.'

'You think she might have told them where . . .'

'No way, honey.' Gradually, the old Babs resumed her place in the driving seat. 'They were her alibi. It wouldn't have been a very good alibi had they known. She was wise. Wise enough to have told some cock-eyed yarn. They'll check. Find it so much hot air.' She stood up from the bed and said, 'Her alibi. *My* alibi, more or less. She was *too* damn clever. Okay, honey, I'll finish the packing. You fix me up with a taxi. Lessford. There'll be a train.' As Liz reached the door, Babs said, 'I – er – I don't want to see anybody else, Liz. All this . . . just between us two.'

'Of course.'

'And – and I won't be back. Ever. Just in case. Tell the kids I love 'em. And Carol. She won't, but ask her . . . give William one more spin when he comes out.'

Old-fashioned, simple-minded tale spinners demand a neatly rounded story; a tale with a beginning, a middle and an end. They are doubly delighted if that end includes a sunset, complete with lovers walking hand-in-hand into a golden future.

But for once the truth . . .

CAROL She became a recluse. Alone, she moved into the Cornish cottage, and in time her everlasting self-pity became such a pain in the neck that even Liz couldn't bring herself to visit. The locals, long-suffering and soft-talking, politely dubbed her eccentric and left her to her ways. One day she will die in the chosen muck and stench of hermitage, and she will die in the firm belief that, through no fault of her own, life has dealt her a lousy and impossible hand.

BABS Babs learned to live with the knowledge that she was a murderess. For a time she drank a little too much and laughed a little too much, but being Babs she eventually came to terms with what she'd done. Her name still rolls up, among the credits at the close of some TV presentation, and sometimes Detective Chief Inspector Hoyle sees, but doesn't notice it. Which of itself is a form of black humour; to know that the officer in charge of the murder enquiry occasionally has the name of the killer beamed into his home but the crime remains undetected.

LIZ She could have married Bryant. It only needed her to stop carrying a torch for an innocent man serving a prison sentence.

Bryant was wise enough to realise this, and had the sense to ease himself out of a situation which would never have really worked. With the departure of Carol, therefore, Liz stayed on to play 'mother' to Robert and Anne. One day William will be free and Liz will be happy to become his Common Law wife, and if prison doesn't break him, but instead *makes* him, it just might result in delayed happiness.

SAL Sal and Robert became engaged. They will one day become man and wife. With the wisdom imparted by Pat, Sal could become an ideal wife . . . despite Oldfield's brainwashing of Robert, and turning him into a jazz buff.

ANNE Anne came out best and, perhaps, deservedly so. That evening at the disco she met the youth she married, after a somewhat whirlwind courtship. A young Post Office worker 'with prospects'. They had nowhere to live, but by that time Carol had disappeared into Cornwall, and they set up home with Liz. It works fine. Rouse was right – the firm preferred money to vengeance – and although Anne's husband may well never re-pay the seventy thousand pounds, so what? It's a good house with good furniture, and it's only like paying rent.

MARY In the Autumn of her life, Mary found her niche. The wife of a good man, tormented by self-guilt beyond his under-standing. But *she* understood, and because she understood, she loved and was happy.

RUTH Who remembers Ruth, other than as an abstract? Other than the creature of some past nightmare? What was left of her was sliced and prodded by a police pathologist, then what was left of *that* went up a crematorium chimney. No mourners, no wreaths, which in a way speaks for itself.

No beginning therefore. No middle. And certainly no neat ending. Just life – a little good, a little bad, for the most part very mediocre – but that's what it's like, and that's how it *was*.